THE STARLET SLUM GIRL

The Victorian Love Sagas
Book 2

Annie Brown

The Starlet Slum Girl — Annie Brown

Copyright © 2024 Annie Brown

The right of Annie Brown identified as the author of this work, has been asserted in accordance with the Copyright Designs and Patents Act 1988.

All rights reserved. No part of this work may be reproduced in any material form (including photocopying or storing by any electronic means and whether or not transiently or incidentally to some other use of this publication) without write permission of the copyright holder except in accordance with the provisions of the Copyright, Designs and Patents Act 1988.

Applications for the copyright holder's permission to reproduce any part of this publication should be addressed to the publishers.

Contents

1. Chapter 1   1
2. Chapter 2   7
3. Chapter 3   13
4. Chapter 4   25
5. Chapter 5   35
6. Chapter 6   38
7. Chapter 7   46
8. Chapter 8   56
9. Chapter 9   61
10. Chapter 10   64
11. Chapter 11   69
12. Chapter 12   74
13. Chapter 13   81
14. Chapter 14   86

15.	Chapter 15	91
16.	Chapter 16	93
17.	Chapter 17	97
18.	Chapter 18	100
19.	Chapter 19	107
20.	Chapter 20	110
21.	Chapter 21	117
22.	Chapter 22	120
23.	Chapter 23	126
24.	Chapter 24	129
25.	Chapter 25	133
26.	Chapter 26	137
27.	Chapter 27	142
28.	Chapter 28	146
29.	Chapter 29	152
30.	Chapter 30	156
31.	Chapter 31	160
32.	Chapter 32	166
33.	Chapter 33	170
34.	Chapter 34	173
35.	Chapter 35	177
36.	Chapter 36	181
37.	Chapter 37	185
38.	Chapter 38	189

39.	Chapter 39	193
Epilogue		199
About the Author		207

Chapter One

※

"What are you all staring at? Get on with your work or no supper for you!" Jenny Franklin's sharp voice echoed through the room, making the children shrink back into their tasks. Jenny's stern gaze swept across each child, checking if any of them dared to take their eyes off their work for a moment.

"Sorry, ma. I just wanted to make sure I'm doing it right," young Nancy stammered, avoiding Jenny's piercing glare.

"Of course you did! I saw you taking a break, trying to avoid work. If you weren't doing it right, I'd tell you. Now, hurry up, all of you! We need these done quick, or no one gets paid!" Jenny scolded; her voice filled with frustration.

"Ouch, Nancy, don't." Dolly whimpered as her older sister kicked her under the table, causing Dolly to retreat in silence as the pain shot up her shin bone.

"You need to pick up the pace, Dolly, or we won't have time to play in the courtyard later. Hurry up. We've got a show to prepare for. You want a part in it don't you?" Nancy urged, her eyes wide with excitement as she looked at her younger sister.

"Yes." Dolly's innocent eyes met Nancy's, filled with hope.

"And less talking from you too, Dolly," Jenny said.

Nancy scowled at her ma, sticking her tongue out behind her back. She couldn't help but feel resentful towards her strict mother, always being hard on her.

"Why is it always me you're picking on? The others talk too, you know." Nancy couldn't hold back her frustration, her words laced with defiance.

"I'll have less of that lip! Don't be cheeky," Jenny reprimanded, her hand swiftly swiping across Nancy's ear.

Nancy's head snapped to the side, her hair falling to cover her face. She couldn't help but imagine a future where she'd be rich and famous, where her ma's harsh treatment would no longer affect her.

"I bet you won't treat me like that when I'm shining under the bright lights of the theatre."

Jenny turned around bewildered at her daughter's audacity.

"You? Rich and famous? In your dreams, young lady. No one would have you, and I ain't surprised," Jenny retorted, shaking her head.

"We'll see." Nancy ducked quickly, narrowly avoiding another slap from her mother. Her siblings continued to work silently, knowing that failing to meet their quota meant no supper.

Hours passed as the children's nimble fingers worked diligently, assembling matchboxes with precision. Piles of completed boxes accumulated on the floor beside each child, the familiar routine etched into their young lives. Folding the frames, sticking the printed paper, and tossing the finished boxes onto the floor—a rhythm they had grown accustomed to.

From eight in the morning till seven at night, the room buzzed with the silent determination of the children. Each crease-free box brought them closer to their meagre wages, the much-anticipated courtyard playtime and, if they were lucky, pigs trotters in their stew.

"I've got an idea! If we don't get more orders, I could sing for our supper. We'd earn plenty to pay rent and put food in our bellies!" Nancy's eyes gleamed with mischief as she dropped a matchbox to the floor.

She climbed onto the bench and then stepped onto the table, twirling around in a makeshift performance. Nancy lifted her dress playfully, her voice resonating with a tune.

'Little Polly Flinders
Sat among the cinders
Warming her pretty little toes
Her Ma came and caught her
And whipped her little daughter
For spoiling her nice new clothes.'

The younger children stared in wonder with their unblinking eyes and mouths wide open and still.

"If you don't stop singing, I'll slap your legs!" Jenny shouted.

Nancy curtsied to the room, her siblings erupting into laughter and cheers.

"See? I told you I could sing for our supper!" Nancy said as her eyes sparkled with a sense of pride.

Her triumph was short-lived as her Ma swiftly caught her and delivered a firm slap to her legs. Nancy sat back down, shaking her head and sticking her tongue out at her brother, Bill, who chuckled and quickly sealed his lips before their ma noticed.

Nancy glanced around the cramped slum house filled with dirty children toiling away. The putrid stench of sewage and dead animals wafted through the open door, mingling with the atmosphere of determination. The light struggled to pierce through the rags stuffed into the cracked windows, a feeble defence against the cold.

"I'll get outta here one day, as far away as possible," Nancy whispered to herself, her eyes glimmering with hope. She dreamed of the limelight, performing on a grand stage in front of hundreds, the applause echoing in her ears.

I'll make sure there's enough for my family too, Nancy vowed, her imagination painting vivid pictures of success and fame. She could almost see her name in lights, gracing the front pages of every newspaper.

"Come on, Nancy. What's taking you so long? You've been on that box for ages. Lost in your dream world again, were you?" Dolly called out, breaking Nancy's reverie.

Jenny stood at the door, her forefinger pointing at each child as she addressed them with a stern gaze. Her words rang in their ears as she set the expectation.

"You all better keep working. No chit-chat or dilly-dallyin', do you 'ere me?"

The children nodded silently, their focus redirected to the task at hand.

When Jenny left the room, slamming the door behind her, Dolly stood up. "You all better keep working. No chit-chat or dilly-dallyin', do you 'ere me?" the young child said mockingly, pointing a finger at each of her siblings and friends as they broke into raucous laughter.

Nancy admired Dolly's confidence, a trait she had gained from their ma and her own experience.

Suddenly, a noise emerged from the corner of the room. Nancy and Dolly stood up quickly to see what had caused the sound.

"Eurgh, look at Sid!" Young Sid had been sick all over his shoes, dribble falling from his mouth as he leant over double. All the other workers started jeering.

"Ew, Sid! I can see yesterday's dinner in there!" Dolly said.

"Quiet you lot, can you not see that he's poorly?" Nancy shouted at the workers.

"Sid, whatever is the matter? Let me help you," Nancy placed her arm around her young brother's shoulder. She could see the pain etched on his pale face.

Sid was doubled over, his arms crossed against his stomach, barely able to walk.

She helped him towards the bedroom, where he vomited once again. The trail of sick resembled a slimy slug, leaving a mark of distress behind him. Dolly, always ready to assist, scurried to get a bucket of hot water and carbolic soap, intent on cleaning up the mess before her ma returned.

Nancy supported Sid as they entered the bedroom, where he collapsed onto the stained sheets, curled up in agony. She wiped his forehead with a damp cloth and looked down on him.

"What's the matter, Sid? You look so pale," Nancy's voice was filled with concern.

Sid didn't have the strength to respond, his eyes closed as he clung to his aching stomach. Nancy held his hand, doing her best to ease his suffering. She looked down at her baby brother wondering how she would cope if he followed her sister, Betty, to an early grave. "Come on, Sid, open your eyes," she said desperately. Nancy exhaled loudly and closed her eyes. The heavy feeling in the pit of her stomach made her fear the worst.

Chapter Two

"Oh, Sid, I'm so worried about you," Nancy said, her voice trembling. Fearful of lurking filth, she questioned if Sid had played in the muddy courtyard. Sid's whimpers of pain were the only response she received, his forehead covered in sweat.

"Did he play in that mud again?" Nancy pondered aloud, her heart heavy with concern.

Without waiting for an answer, she continued to offer comfort to her brother. Nancy's grip tightened on his hand and she wiped the beads of sweat away from his forehead with the back of her hand.

Meanwhile, Dolly diligently scrubbed the floor, erasing any trace of Sid's illness with hot water and carbolic soap.

"Alright, you lot! Get back to work! Ma will be back with her washing, and she won't be happy if she finds you slackin'," Dolly commanded.

The other children glanced at her then, averting their eyes back towards their scar-covered fingers making the small matchboxes.

"Don't give up, Sid," she whispered. Nancy couldn't do much alone, and hoped her ma's presence would ease his suffering.

As Nancy rocked her brother as best she could, her mind wandered to a future beyond the confines of their dreary slum. She daydreamed about the spotlight, the thunderous applause, and the standing ovations she would receive. "Bravo! Bravo, Nancy!" echoed in her imagination as she envisioned herself on the grand stage, basking in the adoration of the audience. Her name would shine in lights outside every theatre in the land.

"Please, Sid, pull through. And I promise I will do everything I can to get us out of here eventually." She held him tight and kissed his forehead as his torso collapsed against hers. The back of his head rested against her chest and she placed a hand over his forehead gently whilst his mouth hung open.

Interrupting her reverie, her ma's voice resonated from the doorway. "Dolly, what's happened here? Why are you on the floor? And where's Sid?"

Dolly ceased her scrubbing and looked up at her Ma, worry etched on her face. "They're in the bedroom, ma. Sid's not feeling well."

Jenny dropped her basket, the clean laundry cascading onto the floor. Her focus shifted immediately to her ailing son as she rushed into the bedroom. Nancy, ever vigilant, stepped aside to allow her ma access to her youngest son.

"I'm sorry, ma. It happened so fast. One moment he was working, and the next, he was sick," Nancy explained, her voice filled with worry.

Jenny took hold of Sid's hand, her touch gentle yet urgent. "Don't worry, Nancy. You did well, lass. Taking care of him like that," she murmured, her words a gentle balm to Nancy's worried heart.

Nancy sank down onto the bed beside her ma, her arm reaching around Dolly's shoulders who had joined them. She offered solace to her younger sister, who sought comfort by sucking her thumb. All eyes were fixated on Sid, their unspoken prayers weaving a web of hope.

"He's gonna be fine, Nancy. We won't entertain any other thoughts," Jenny said, trying to quell her own rising panic. Her words were meant to soothe her daughter, though deep down, she too struggled with doubt.

The room fell into a tense hush, each breath heavy with worry. They anxiously waited for Sid's recovery, not wanting to lose a beloved family member.

Just as hope and fear danced on the fragile thread of uncertainty, a sound shattered the silence. Arthur stumbled in noisily. His A-board slipping from his grasp.

"Hello? Anybody home?" Arthur called out, his eyes scanning the empty room for his wife and children. Confusion washed over him, wondering why there was no one around.

Jenny's voice led him to the bedroom, calling out, "Arthur, in here!"

"Ah, I found you all," Arthur said, noticing Sid's weakened state.

He rushed over, dropping to his knees beside the bed, placing one hand on Sid's forehead. The heat radiating from his son's skin was cause for alarm. Arthur's other hand rested on Jenny's arm, attempting to offer solace amidst their shared concern.

"What happened? How long has he been like this?" Arthur's voice quivered with worry, his eyes searching Jenny's face for answers.

"About an hour and a half, pa." One minute he was working, and the next, he was sick everywhere," Nancy replied, her voice tinged with unease.

"I was just in the courtyard fetching the washing. Didn't expect this to happen," Jenny said, her voice a mix of exhaustion and worry. She slumped onto the threadbare eiderdown, her tears staining her worn dress.

Arthur offered a weak smile to Jenny, blinking away his own apprehension. He turned to Nancy, his eyes filled with gratitude.

"You did good, Nancy. Both you and Dolly. Lookin' after him," Arthur said, his words a small solace amid their turmoil.

Nancy nodded, accepting her father's praise silently. She knew she had done her best to care for Sid, even as uncertainty loomed. Their shared hope and fear intertwined as they held vigil by Sid's side.

"Pa, do you think Sid—" Nancy's voice wavered, her concern palpable.

"Don't even say those words, Nancy. Little Sid here is gonna be just fine, aren't you, lad?" Arthur asked, his voice filled with a father's desperate hope. Yet Sid remained unresponsive.

"Nancy, do me a favour, love. Tell the other workers they can leave. We don't want anyone else falling ill, and we ain't sure if this thing is contagious. It's hard enough with one worker down. We need to make sure the rest'll come back tomorrow," Jenny instructed, her voice heavy with worry and responsibility.

Nancy made her way back to the workroom, her thoughts swirling with fear and the weight of her family's future. The room, previously filled with children's chatter, was now eerily still. She approached each child, delivering the news with a heavy heart.

"You can all go home. Leave your boxes here, we'll count them later and make sure you get paid. See you tomorrow, alright?" Nancy's words lacked their usual cheer, replaced by a sombre tone that hung in the air.

Without a word, the children filed out, their eyes filled with concern for Sid. Jenny's mind was too preoccupied to count the boxes, her focus solely on her ailing son. The evening grew darker, the slum house cloaked in worry, awaiting the dawn and the answers it might bring.

Arthur's arrival had shattered the tense air, momentarily filling the room with hope. But as he beheld his son's frail form, the weight of uncertainty settled upon his shoulders. He gathered Jenny into his embrace, their tears mingling with their shared fears.

"There, there, Jenny. Let's not jump to conclusions, alright? This might pass before mornin'," Arthur whispered, his words an attempt to calm his wife's frayed nerves, even as his own faith wavered.

Nancy, feeling the need to lighten the heavy atmosphere, spoke up, her voice filled with a hint of cheerfulness.

"Pa, would you like to hear my new song? I learned it today, heard other children singing it," Nancy offered, hoping to bring a moment of respite to her worried parents.

"Yes, why not," Arthur said, seeking an approving nod from his wife. "But sing softly, love. We wouldn't want Sid to be startled awake. Who knows, a nice tune might just help him feel better."

Nancy stood up from the bed, curtsying gracefully to her father before beginning her song.

'Little Polly Flinders
Sat among the cinders
Warming her pretty little toes
Her Ma came and caught her
And whipped her little daughter

For spoiling her nice new clothes.'

Finishing her song, Nancy curtsied once more, awaiting her father's response.

"I think you're wonderful, Nancy. And your ma does too, don't you, Jenny?" A glimmer of pride shining in his eyes.

"You'll be up on that stage one day, Nancy. I just know it," Arthur added, his words carrying a mix of encouragement and paternal affection.

As his smile faded, Arthur turned his attention back to Sid, noticing a change in his breathing. "See, Nancy? Your singing has calmed him. He'll thank you for that."

Nancy settled back onto the bed, pulling Dolly closer to her side. Their shared worry and weariness forged a silent bond. Meanwhile, all eyes remained fixed on the sick boy. The young boy's family prayed for his recovery as the gloomy slum room descended into restless slumber.

Chapter Three

The rain poured as the Franklins gathered by Sid's grave, a sombre scene on that wet September day. They wore their best clothes, despite a few patched holes and stains here and there. Nancy had even mended Dolly's dress. Jenny and Arthur stood hand in hand, while Nancy, Dolly, and Bill watched in silence. They didn't know what to say to comfort their grieving parents. Losing two children in just three months left Nancy wondering if her parents were anticipating another tragedy. How could they not, after experiencing such losses? Nancy watched as her Ma buried her face into her father's neck, sobbing uncontrollably. He stood there, red-eyed, with an arm draped around her shoulder trying his best to be strong for the family.

"We'll get through this, my love, you'll see," her father whispered, his lips moving without sound.

Nancy held her father's hand tightly, her own eyes welling up with tears and her grief locked within her body and soul. Her heart ached more than she would allow to show as she wondered which of her siblings would be taken next. She watched as her father wiped away his red-stained eyes with his left hand. He longed to be strong for his family, but his knees felt weak and his tears flowed unabated. Their youngest son now rested among paupers' graves, without even a headstone to mark his place. Instead, they each plucked a flower from the nearby park and dropped it onto his final resting spot.

They stood there by the grave, time stretching on like an eternity. The drizzle persisted, and Jenny seemed rooted to the spot.

"If I leave now Arthur, then I've left him for good, haven't I?" she asked, her voice trembling with grief. She knew that once she left the graveyard, visits would be few and far between. The need to put food on the table and pay the rent to keep her family alive and warm was greater than visiting her son who had passed.

Each time she spoke, tears streamed down her face, and her children watched on feeling hopeless. They loved all their siblings, but Jenny knew that this loss would be harder to overcome. Sid, had almost died at birth. When he took his first breath, after the doctor held him upside down and spanked his legs, it was nothing short of a miracle. God was looking down on them that day, but today he felt vacant in their hearts.

"Ma's little miracle and ray of sunshine, that's what you are, Sid. You've made your ma a very happy lady," she used to say as she tickled him under the chin. He spent many of his early days wrapped up in a cloth against her belly as she did the washing in the sewage-covered courtyard.

Nancy felt like hours had passed as they made their way back to the slums. Jenny clung to Arthur for support, stumbling every time the weight of their son's loss overwhelmed her. Nancy remembered the night Sid fell ill, her Ma desperately begging him not to go.

"Don't go, Sid. Don't you dare leave us now!" she had pleaded, her voice filled with desperation.

Nancy had to leave the room, unable to bear witness to her Ma's overwhelming display of love. It was something the eldest child felt she had never received from her. Instead, she endured her Ma's verbal abuse, berated for talking too much or for dancing and singing on the table when she should have been working. The constant barrage of criticism made her feel useless and unloved.

"But please, ma, I'm just trying to cheer you up," Nancy would defend herself.

Jenny's response was always harsh. "I tell you what would cheer me up—you doing the bloody work like I ask. Now, get to it!"

Her words were often followed by a stinging slap across the back of Nancy's legs.

As they made their way back to the slums, the market stallholders and passers-by noticed their grief, a heavy weight of loss etched upon their faces. The men doffed their hats, and the women stood still with their heads bowed, casting their gaze to the ground.

The heartbroken family walked through the imposing gates into the courtyard, where their fellow slum dwellers had formed a line in the pouring rain to welcome them home. Jenny and Arthur moved along the line, shaking hands with each impoverished neighbour. No words were exchanged, only nods and vacant expressions that spoke volumes.

"I have tea and leftover gingerbread for you and the family, Jenny. It should be good enough to eat," Betty from the floor above said. Arthur followed the two women inside, unsure of how else to comfort his wife.

"Do you want to play outside, kids?" Arthur asked, turning his attention to Nancy, Dolly, and Bill.

They nodded in unison, eager for a brief respite from their parents' sorrow. As they watched their ma and pa disappear inside, seeking refuge from the dark and gloomy drizzle, Dolly and Bill sat on upturned tea chests, looking to Nancy for guidance.

"What shall we do, Nancy?" Dolly asked, her eyes fixed on her older sister as she toyed with a piece of wood between her nimble fingers.

"If it were up to me, I'd practise putting on a show. Sid may have died, but the show must go on. Pa's birthday is coming up, and the best gift we can give him is a show from the three of us. What do you say?" Nancy suggested.

Her younger siblings nodded, waiting for Nancy to take the lead. Rising to her feet, she gathered the hem of her dress and climbed atop an empty crate.

"Ladies and gentlemen, please welcome to the stage, Miss Nancy Franklin!" Nancy declared, adopting the role of a mock compere. Dolly and Bill clapped and cheered, joining in the excitement. Nancy paid no mind to the judgmental gazes of the other drunken slum dwellers. She could almost hear their muttered words:

"How disgraceful those children are for singing and dancing today."

But Nancy persisted.

"Have you seen enough yet?" Nancy called out, directing her attention toward Maggie from the neighbouring slum, who always complained about the noise the Franklin family made.

THE STARLET SLUM GIRL

"Yeah, that's right! I bet you're not complaining now, are you, you old bag?" Nancy taunted, sticking her tongue out. Maggie turned away in disgust whilst Nancy stood in front of her siblings and pretended she was on stage. Her younger siblings curtsied and bowed respectively, pretending they were performing in front of a grand audience. Nancy directed them to sing together.

'Here we go round the mulberry bush,
The mulberry bush,
The mulberry bush.
Here we go round the mulberry bush
On a cold and frosty morning.'

The three filthy children leaped off the crates and danced in a circle. Nancy held her hair back, as if performing for an imaginary audience.

This is the way we wash our face,
Wash our face,
Wash our face.
This is the way we wash our face
On a cold and—'

"Have you no respect?" a stern voice interrupted. "I expected better from you three, given that you just buried Sid."

Dolly pursed her lips, and Bill clutched Nancy's hand, seeking solace in her presence. The children looked towards the voice, and there stood Betty, her gaze filled with disapproval. Betty, who lived upstairs, stared at them long enough to convey her disappointment, then stomped off toward the slum house, casting one final cold, hard stare at Nancy.

Nancy stood frozen in place, her body trembling, anticipating the punishment that awaited her from her ma.

"Don't worry, Nancy. We'll take the blame too, won't we, Bill?" Dolly said, her eyes wide with determination, making sure her younger brother understood his role.

"Oh well, the show must go on! Right, Dolly, Bill, where were we?" Nancy mustered a brave smile, determined to salvage the moment.

"No, Dolly, not there. Nancy wants you to stand here instead of next to me. That's right, isn't it, Nancy?" Bill chimed in, his young voice astute.

"Very good, Bill. Spot on. You'll be a stage director before you know it!" Nancy praised him with a playful smile and a glint in her eyes.

"But, Nancy, I want to play the lead part," Dolly pouted, her thumb finding solace in her mouth, eyes downcast.

"It's not fair, Nancy. You always get the biggest part," she complained.

"That's because I'm the eldest, silly. Young children can't play the main part in shows," Nancy explained, trying to reason with her younger sister.

"Oh, yes, they can!" Dolly defiantly declared, shoving Nancy, causing her to lose her balance and fall backward onto the filthy ground.

"Now look what you've done, Dolly! I'm going to get into so much trouble for that!" Nancy stood up and tried to brush the dirt off her dress.

But instead of retaliating and adopting her ma's harsh, dictatorial mannerisms, Nancy knelt down to Dolly's level and embraced her. "You shouldn't do that, Dolly. It's not nice."

"I'm sorry, Nancy. I didn't mean to do it," Dolly whimpered, remorse filling her voice.

"Come on, let's try again!" Nancy said, offering a forgiving smile.

The children hadn't noticed a gentleman standing by the gates. He had observed their performance for nearly half an hour, his gaze fixed intently on Nancy. Lighting a cigarette, he exhaled a perfect smoke ring into the air.

"She's the one," he murmured, extinguishing his cigarette and dropping it to the damp ground.

"Bravo! Bravo!" he applauded, as he approached the makeshift stage.

The other slum dwellers paused in their activities and looked up, curious about the stranger's next move.

"Bravo!" he repeated, reaching the children and standing before them. "That was a great performance, have you been practicing for long?"

Bill moved closer to Nancy, seeking shelter, while Dolly hid timidly behind her sister, peeking out from the side of Nancy's skirt, clutching it tightly. She had heard of children being snatched, destined for the workhouse. Those tales scared her, and she didn't want to suffer the same fate.

"There, there, little one. I'm not going to hurt you," the stranger reassured, extending a comforting hand toward the trembling trio.

With synchronised caution, the children took a step back. "Don't come near us. You stay away," Nancy warned, her voice filled with protective determination.

"I'm not going to hurt you," the stranger insisted.

Maggie, who worked at the slum shop, noticed the commotion and hastily abandoned her laundry, rushing to the Franklins' room. Urgently knocking on the door, she peered around the corner to make sure the children were still there.

Bang, bang, bang!

Arthur's weary voice resonated through the room. "I'm coming." He had just removed his arm from beneath Jenny, who had fallen asleep in the midst of her tears. Stirred awake, he stomped over to the entrance, letting out a deep sigh.

"We want nothing," he called out, his tone weary. "We are mourning the death of little Sid. Now, if you would just—"

He swung open the door, startled to see Maggie standing there, no time to inquire further.

"Hurry, Arthur! There's a man talking to the bairns," she blurted, and then rushed back to the courtyard without waiting for a response.

Arthur followed suit, not bothering to put his boots back on. He dashed across the courtyard, slipping and sliding in the mud.

"Oi, who are you? Get away!" Arthur shouted, waving his protective arms at the stranger as his children watched on, wide-eyed.

"I said get away, leave them alone! I've already lost two children, and I won't be losing any more! You're not taking them!" Arthur ran as fast as he could, but his momentum sent him crashing down onto the muddy ground. He clumsily pulled himself up, leaning on an empty barrel for support.

"I said, leave my kids alone!" he panted, his words barely intelligible through his breathlessness.

The stranger approached slowly, trying to calm the situation. "What did you think I was going to do? Kidnap them?"

"You won't be able to do anything, because I won't give you the chance. Now, get lost. I don't want to see you around here again!" Arthur said.

"You might think differently when you hear what I've got to say," the stranger replied calmly.

Arthur tried to compose himself and tucked his shirt back into his trousers. He couldn't help but feel inferior standing in front of the impeccably dressed stranger.

"Aye? What's that, then?"

The stranger smiled, glancing at Nancy. "This child here, is she yours?"

"What's it to you?" Arthur retorted.

The stranger moved closer, placing an arm around all three children as best he could. "I want her to sing for me. I've been watching her perform, and she's very talented."

Nancy shifted her gaze between the stranger and her father, a flicker of excitement igniting within her.

"Pa! Pa, please!" she pleaded, tugging at his shirt, her actions threatening to untuck it once again. Arthur took hold of her hand, his eyes fixed on the stranger.

"What do you mean you want her to sing? She's only sixteen, you know. She's not old enough for that sort of thing yet."

"They all start young, Mr ..." the stranger hesitated.

Arthur responded, "Franklin, Arthur Franklin is my name."

Thank you Mr Franklin, my name is Alex Compton, and I'm a talent scout of the good, old-fashioned variety. I'm always on the lookout for talents like your Nancy here."

"How do you know her name?" Arthur asked, suspicion creeping into his voice.

The stranger smiled warmly. "Your children have been calling each other by their names the whole time I've been watching."

"So, where will she be singing then? I hope it's not some dodgy place. I've heard stories about what goes on in those music halls. Men paying women for... extras, if you catch my drift," Arthur suggested, concern etched on his face.

"Oh, Mr Franklin, I'm talking about proper shows! Stage productions where people pay good money to see actors and actresses like your daughter. She could be a star, you know."

Nancy's stage presence appealed to Arthur, who daydreamed about a struggle-free life for his family. There would be no more selling matchboxes and worrying about rent or food. The possibilities for his family's future seemed endless.

"So, what do you say, then? Is it a yes or a no?" Alex Compton inquired, extending his hand toward Arthur.

Arthur looked at Mr Compton, then at Nancy, who was practically bouncing with anticipation, her eyes shining brightly.

"Please, pa! This could be me' one and only chance!" Nancy pleaded, her voice filled with hope and determination.

Arthur's eyebrows furrowed, weighing the risks and rewards of the stranger's proposition. The decision had the potential to change their lives, but he feared Jenny's wrath for deciding without her.

"How much will you pay her, then?" Arthur finally asked, his voice tinged with cautious optimism.

Alex Compton smiled, seeing the flicker of interest in Arthur's eyes. "Let's start with two pounds a week. That should do it, Mr Franklin."

The children's mouths fell open wide, their eyebrows furrowing together.

Nancy crossed her fingers tightly behind her back and screwed her eyes shut praying for her pa to give the answer she so desperately wanted to hear.

"Done!" Arthur exclaimed, his hands reaching out to shake Alec's. The deal was sealed, and a surge of excitement coursed through him.

"When will she start?" Arthur inquired eagerly, unable to hide his enthusiasm.

"How about two weeks' time? That will give you all a chance to prepare a show for your birthday, Arthur – if I may call you that? I'm sure you'll enjoy it," Alec suggested, his eyes gleaming with a hint of mischief.

Nancy gasped, realising that the surprise show they had planned for their father's birthday had been exposed. She shot a reproachful glance at Alec.

"It was supposed to be a surprise. Why did you go and tell him?" Nancy protested, feeling a mix of annoyance and anticipation.

Alec chuckled apologetically. "My mistake. I didn't know it was a secret. Now, if you'll excuse me, I must be on my way. You'll hear from me in a few days, Nancy, about when and where I want you to perform."

With that, Alec turned on his heels and walked tentatively out of the courtyard, taking care to avoid the muddy patches.

The children giggled, watching him lift his trousers and tiptoe cautiously to preserve his cleanliness.

"Two whole pounds a week, eh? That'll pay the rent and put food on the table," Arthur mused aloud, his mind racing with visions of a brighter future. He couldn't help but imagine Nancy's face gracing the front pages of newspapers, their family basking in newfound prosperity. No more matchboxes, no more struggle.

"Now I just have to tell your mother. Maybe I should wait until tomorrow," Arthur pondered, his voice laced with a touch of apprehension.

"I think you should wait, pa. She's too upset to hear the good news right now," Nancy suggested, her voice filled with empathy.

Arthur rubbed Nancy's head affectionately, grateful for her understanding. "Right, come on, you three. Let's go and get some supper. It's been a long, hard day, and I'm hungry."

As they entered their dingy, downtrodden slum, Arthur glanced at Jenny, lost in her grief. He couldn't help but feel a twinge of guilt for the secret he was harbouring, knowing that it would bring both joy and apprehension to his wife. But the stage awaited Nancy, and the journey ahead would test their family's strength and resilience in ways they could never have imagined.

Chapter Four

Nancy's graceful curtsy garnered a round of applause, and her father, watching from the audience, beamed with joy.

"Bravo! Bravo! Bravo!" The gentlemen in the crowd doffed their hats, while the ladies smiled at their husbands, trying to divert their attention from the captivating young woman standing on stage in her splendid makeup and costume.

"She may be only seventeen, but she looks at least twenty-five!" remarked one gentleman.

"You're right, Jack. I'd take her as my wife any day!" chimed in another.

Nancy's father winced at the comments from the men beside him, but he knew that someday he would have to let his daughter spread her wings and soar. She was the most talented member of their family, with the greatest potential. Ever since she started performing at the Eagle Tavern, Nancy had been bringing home a substantial income. Two pounds a week supplemented their meagre earnings from matchboxes, ensuring they could pay the rent on time, put food on the table, and even afford a few luxuries.

Arthur longed to give up the matchbox business, but he knew it was impossible until Nancy made it on the big stage. They needed the money, and without it, they would be homeless.

"More! More!" the crowd shouted. "We want more, Nancy!"

Nancy winked and blew kisses at the crowd. The men felt a stirring in their hearts, whilst the women looked away in disapproval. Men were taken away by their wives to stop them from staring.

Nancy left the stage after the crowd dispersed, unaware of a gentleman sitting at the back. He sat with his legs crossed, lighting a cigarette and releasing smoke rings into the air. Unnoticed by Nancy, her father brushed past him, oblivious to the stranger awaiting his daughter's reappearance.

"What did you think, Leo? Was I alright?" Nancy asked, seeking validation from her close friend.

"You were more than alright, Nancy Franklin. You were wonderful," Leo said, standing behind the tall, dark-haired Nancy as she settled in front of her makeshift mirror. Yet, it served its purpose for now. A mirror balanced on an empty barrel, accompanied by a hard-backed chair, provided enough space for Nancy and Leo as he helped her remove the heavy costumes. Leo had become a constant presence in her life since her first performance at the Eagle Tavern.

"I can spot talent when I see it," he had told her on her debut night. "It's as if you've been doing this your whole life."

"Like what you see, huh?" Nancy replied, realising that Leo's interests lay more in costume making than anything carnal. Nevertheless, he was an excellent designer. Countless nights were spent at Leo's house, where they shared dreams of wealth and success. Nancy, the performer, and Leo, her confidante and costume maker.

"Nancy, I believe your lucky break is just around the corner. I can feel it," Leo said enthusiastically. "I can already picture your name in lights, shining brightly in front of a deep red velvet curtain." As he spoke, Leo's hands gracefully arched through the air, painting a vivid image of grandeur.

"You can't keep performing here for a mere two pounds a week. It won't make us millionaires."

"But, Leo, I love it here," Nancy responded, swatting his hand away. "The lively audience always wants more. At least I know I'll have a decent crowd. I don't have to worry about performing to empty seats. Besides, the more they drink, the more money they throw at me."

Leo placed his hands on Nancy's shoulders. "You, my dear, are destined for fame. Soon, the national newspapers will be singing your praises, not just the local gossip."

"Oh, Leo, don't tease," Nancy said, playfully slapping his hand. "Where am I going to find someone to help me achieve that? No talent scout in their right mind would venture to these parts of London!"

"You never know, Nancy. One night, a scout more suited to your talent than Alex might be in the audience, waiting to sign you up."

The stranger at the back of the theatre, hidden from Nancy's sight, observed the young starlet with keen interest. Her father, Arthur, approached the man, oblivious to the fact that the stranger was waiting for his daughter.

"I haven't seen you around here before. Have you lived here long?" Arthur asked, his curiosity piqued.

The stranger took a slow drag on his cigarette before looking at Arthur. "I'm not from around here. I live on the other side of the city in Holly Village. A place quite different from Whitechapel. Robert Wheeler, pleased to meet you," Robert said, moving his shaking hand towards Arthur's.

"Holly Village, eh? What brings you to these parts, then?" Arthur said, as he glanced at Robert's hand and ignored his handshake.

"Nancy, the performer. I heard she's worth watching, so I decided to take a trip and see what she's all about."

Arthur considered whether the well-dressed man had ulterior motives, wondering if he was making advances towards his daughter. Despite Nancy being seventeen, he still wanted to ensure she didn't fall in with the wrong crowd. Arthur decided to assess the stranger's intentions and protect Nancy's well-being.

"Is that so? What did you like about her performance? I watch every show, and each one feels different to me."

"Well, she possesses a remarkable voice, and she knows how to captivate the crowd. But Nancy differs from the rest. She has a certain charm, don't you think? It's something you can't practice or fake. She has a natural ability to draw people towards her, without resorting to the usual tricks most performers employ."

"You're right. It's one thing I admire most about her. She's a true gem, our Nancy," Arthur responded with pride.

The stranger uncrossed his legs and sat up in his chair, extinguishing his cigarette on the floor with a twist of his polished brogue. The barman, witnessing the act, was far from pleased. Mopping the floor again would result in a penny deduction from his wages. The stranger met the barman's gaze, silently conveying a message of "do it yourself, you're paid for it."

"Now, where were we? Ah, yes, Nancy," the stranger resumed, extending his hand towards Arthur. "I'm a talent scout, a manager if you will, always on the lookout for new stars to grace the Adelphi stage. Good performers are hard to come by these days, and when I spot one, I don't let them go until they've become a star."

"Glad to hear that!" Arthur responded with a hearty, working-class laugh. "I'm Arthur Franklin, and I've been watching and supporting Nancy since her very first night. Please forgive my wariness, though. The last scout let her down. He promised her the world and then left when he got a better offer."

"That's not how I do business, Mr Franklin. Far from it," the stranger assured. "When I find someone as talented as Nancy, I stick by them until they shine."

"I'm pleased to hear that," Arthur replied, his scepticism fading away.

"Pa, there you are! How was my performance tonight?" Nancy emerged from the shadows and approached her father. Leo trailed close behind, wearing a smile on his face.

"I told her, Mr Franklin, she's destined to be a true star! She just won't believe me," Leo chimed in.

"I think she should start believing, don't you, Mr Wheeler?" Arthur said, gesturing towards the stranger seated at the table.

Nancy and Leo turned their attention to the man in the chair, hidden from the bright, bare lightbulbs. Nancy found herself unable to look away as their eyes locked. She felt an instant connection and an overwhelming curiosity to learn more.

"And who might you be? You're lingering quite late, aren't you? I'm sure a handsome gentleman like you must have a wife waiting at home," Nancy said, her gaze fixed on Robert.

"Nancy, where are your manners?" Arthur scolded.

"I'm just curious why he's still here, pa," Nancy responded, her eyes still locked with Robert's.

"My name is Robert Wheeler, and I might just be the one to make you a star," Robert declared, taking Nancy's hand and pressing a gentle kiss to it.

A wave of excitement coursed through Nancy's body, and she couldn't help but smile. She glanced back at Leo, while Robert's words made her feel like royalty. Leo, however, crossed his arms and frowned, clearly not as enthused.

"So, what's your plan, then?" Nancy inquired, her curiosity piqued.

"Well, first, to answer your earlier question, no, I don't have a wife. I'm still waiting for that special someone to spend the rest of my life with. As for you, how about joining me for a late supper? I can share why I believe you should hire me as your manager," Robert suggested.

Nancy glanced at her father and Leo, seeking their approval. Robert quickly intervened before they could respond.

"Of course, your friend and your father are more than welcome to accompany us if it makes you feel safer," Robert assured her.

Nancy's father weighed the situation, realising that Leo's presence would ensure Nancy's safety. He handed the stranger a knowing look. "Nancy, why don't you let Leo join you? I need to get home to your ma and see if she's still talking to me after having another late night. Leo, please make sure she gets home safely."

Leo nodded begrudgingly, knowing he could use an early night himself. He didn't want to get in the way of Nancy and the man who had caught her eye.

"Sure thing, Mr Franklin. I'll make sure she gets home," Leo agreed.

"Oh, pa, you make it sound like I'm fourteen again," Nancy said.

Robert sought to ease Arthur's concerns and align himself with the protective father figure. "Your father is right, Nancy. You've only just met me, and it's essential to consider your safety in these streets of Whitechapel."

Nancy rolled her eyes. "Oh, alright then. Let's go and eat something. I'll see you later, pa. Send my love to ma and the kids."

Nancy, Robert, and Leo exited the tavern, with Arthur heading in a different direction. Robert led the way, Nancy and Leo following in the shadows.

"Leo, I hope he's paying. I've spent all my money on rent and feathers," Nancy whispered to her friend.

"Quiet now, Nancy. We've just met the man. I'm sure he wouldn't have invited us if he didn't intend to pay," Leo responded, playfully jabbing his friend in the ribs.

Suddenly, Robert stopped, causing Nancy and Leo to stop abruptly.

"Of course, I'll pay. Why wouldn't I pay for a young woman as magnificent as Nancy Franklin?" Robert declared, taking her hand once more and planting a soft kiss on it.

Leo nudged Nancy again, showing that she had found herself a generous companion. Nancy blushed, looking behind at Leo, who folded his arms and frowned.

"Well, I'm being spoiled tonight. Thank you, Robert. I could get used to this," Nancy remarked.

"In that case, my dear, you'll have no trouble taking the lead role in our upcoming shows," Robert suggested, a mischievous twinkle in his eyes.

Nancy wiggled her shoulders and swayed her hips. "Robert, you're already charming me."

Leo couldn't help but interject. "Stop it!" he murmured, catching up with Nancy and Robert.

"Here we are, climb aboard!" Robert gestured towards a Brougham carriage.

Nancy raised an eyebrow, looking at Robert with curiosity. "Robert, where are we going?"

"You'll see," he replied, offering her his arm. Nancy linked her hand through his, Leo trailing behind with a hint of sulkiness. The carriage set off through the bustling streets of London, arriving at their destination outside a grand restaurant near Hyde Park.

Nancy's eyes widened in awe as she stepped out of the carriage and looked up at the establishment. Robert, observing her reaction, realised she had experienced nothing quite like it. He placed a hand on his hip, inviting Nancy to link her arm with his.

"May I?" Robert asked, and Nancy eagerly obliged, entwining her arm with his. Leo followed behind, his sulking forgotten when the head waiter gave him a wink and a nod, signalling their arrival at the table.

Nancy gazed upward, taking in the affluent crowd enjoying their supper with loved ones. Amidst the revelry, she observed some couples having more fun than others.

"This place is rather posh, isn't it? What is this, anyway?" Nancy inquired, her eyes darting around the restaurant.

"This, Nancy Franklin, is the Adelphi Theatre restaurant. If everything goes well with your future performances, you could be dining here every night," Robert explained.

Nancy wriggled in her seat and shook her hips from side to side. "Well, if it means enjoying this regularly, count me in. What do you think, Leo?"

She glanced at her friend, who seemed preoccupied elsewhere. "Oi, Leo, what do you think?"

"What? Sorry? Yes, I agree," Leo replied, tearing his gaze away from the head waiter in the corner and joining the conversation.

"What are you agreeing with, Leo? You haven't heard a word I've said."

"I agree with you, as long as it involves me making more costumes and chaperoning you to your shows."

Nancy looked at Robert and smiled. "You heard the man. As long as he comes along, then you've got yourself a brand-new performer."

"I'll drink to that!" Robert exclaimed, raising his glass and tapping it against Nancy's, their eyes locked in a shared moment of excitement. They savoured their meal, washing it down with champagne, their laughter filling the air.

"This is delicious, Robert. I could get used to this," Nancy remarked, her eyes sparkling with delight.

"And get used to it you shall," Robert responded with a confident grin. "You're destined for greatness, Nancy. A real star in the making."

As Nancy and Leo looked around, they couldn't ignore the gazes fixed upon them. The whispers and curious glances from other diners made Nancy momentarily self-conscious.

"Either they recognise me from somewhere or they think I don't belong here," Nancy mused.

"Nonsense," Robert reassured her. "Don't be too hard on yourself. You're better than you think you are."

Their food arrived, and they continued their meal, enjoying every bite. The night felt like a dream with flowing champagne. Nancy couldn't help but feel a sense of belonging in Robert's company.

"You know, Robert," Nancy said, leaning in closer, "this has been an incredible evening. I can't wait to see what the future holds."

Robert's eyes sparkled with a mix of admiration and ambition. "And I promise you, Nancy, together we'll conquer the world. You'll be a shining star."

Leo, however, still had reservations as he observed the interaction between Nancy and Robert. He glanced at the head waiter, who caught his eye once more, leading to a subtle exchange of gestures.

"Oh, excuse me?" Leo called out to the waiter.

"Yes, sir?" the waiter responded, approaching their table.

"A bottle of your finest champagne, please," Leo requested, a mischievous glimmer in his eyes.

The waiter nodded, amused by Leo's antics. "Very well, sir. I'll bring it right away."

Nancy nudged Leo. "Leo, what are you up to?"

He grinned mischievously. "Just adding a little extra sparkle to our evening. May aswell make the most of it seeing that your new beau is paying."

As the night continued, laughter filled the air, and the champagne flowed freely. Nancy's heart raced with excitement, knowing that her life was about to change forever. And little did she know, fate had a surprise in store for her, one that would test her resolve and challenge her dreams.

Chapter Five

Nancy's heart swelled with anticipation as Robert's carriage disappeared into the night, carrying him away from her slum house. Nancy burst through the door, her heart still racing from the exhilaration of her performance. She could hardly contain her excitement as she called out to her Ma, Jenny.

Yet, as she stepped back into the room, her Ma's disapproving gaze greeted her.

"You stayed out late, didn't you? Where have you been?" Jenny asked, her foot tapping impatiently.

"I was out, ma. With a gentleman who believes in my talent and wants to make me a star," Nancy responded, a glimmer of hope in her voice.

Jenny was unimpressed. "Still holding on to those lofty dreams, are you? You'd be better off working here, making these matchboxes." Jenny's eyes narrowed, her expression a mix of anger and concern. "Nancy, I've told you before, the stage isn't a place for a respectable girl."

Nancy's enthusiasm wavered for a moment. Her shoulders slumped as she faced her Ma's disapproval head-on. But a fire ignited within her, fuelled by years of yearning for something more than their suffocating environment.

"Ma, you don't understand. The stage is my passion, my calling. I can't deny the pull it has on my soul," Nancy asserted, her voice filled with determination.

Jenny's eyes hardened, her voice taking on a sharp edge. "Passion won't put food on the table or keep a roof over our heads. I've seen too many dreams dashed, too many girls lost to the harsh realities of that world. I won't let you be another casualty."

A mix of anger and sorrow surged through Nancy. She loved her Ma, but she couldn't let her own dreams wither away under the weight of Jenny's fears.

"Ma, I respect your concerns, but I can't ignore the fire that burns within me. I won't let fear hold me back from pursuing what I love," Nancy said, her voice filled with defiance as she grabbed her coat. "And besides, my weekly contribution seems to have done us well so far, don't you think?"

Jenny's face flushed with anger, her voice trembling with frustration. "If you walk out that door tonight, Nancy, don't bother coming back. I won't have a daughter of mine disgracing our family."

Nancy's heart pounded in her chest as she looked at her Ma, her gaze unwavering. She knew the stakes, the sacrifices that lay before her. But she couldn't let her dreams be extinguished by the weight of familial expectations.

With a determined glint in her eyes, Nancy defied her Ma's wishes and rushed towards the door, her voice filled with determination.

"I'm sorry, but I can't let your fears and worries dampen the fire within me. I have to follow my dreams, no matter the consequences," Nancy said, her voice firm.

Jenny watched her daughter step out into the night. A mixture of anger, sorrow, and a Ma's love warred within her, creating a whirlwind of conflicting emotions.

As the door slammed shut, Jenny sank to her knees, tears streaming down her face. She had tried to protect her daughter, to shield her from the pitfalls of the stage, but she couldn't deny the ache in her heart. She knew deep down that Nancy was destined for something greater, even if it meant defying her and the safety of their home.

Jenny's inner conflict intensified as she watched her daughter leave. She was torn between her desire to keep Nancy safe and pride in her daughter's unwavering determination. The future remained uncertain and the consequences of Nancy's rebellion were, as yet, unknown. But one thing was clear—Nancy had chosen her path, and Jenny was left to grapple with the consequences of her daughter's defiance.

Meanwhile, Arthur listened to the sound of the door slamming, his heart heavy with worry. Had he just witnessed the last of his precious daughter?

Chapter Six

"Extra! Extra! Read all about it! Hey mister, want a copy? Thanks a bunch! Have a splendid day!" The scruffy young lad called out, exchanging the gentleman's money for a copy of the Daily Telegraph.

He continued his lively shouts, hoping to attract passers-by and convince them to part with their pennies for a peek at the day's news. Meanwhile, the well-dressed gentleman strolled down the street, unrolling the newspaper and immersing himself in the front-page headlines.

The bold letters screamed out the news.

"NANCY FRANKLIN WOWS ADELPHI THEATRE GOERS!"

> "NANCY FRANKLIN TAKES ADELPHI THEATRE BY STORM WITH HER DEBUT!"

> "NANCY FRANKLIN'S DAZZLING PERFORMANCE EARNS STANDING OVATION AND ENCORES!"

> "NANCY FRANKLIN'S STAR ON THE RISE THANKS TO MANAGER, ROBER WHEELER!"

The man licked his lips, lost in thought about his next move. He headed towards the Strand, newspaper rolled up under his arm, and decided to have lunch at the Adelphi Theatre restaurant. There, he could sit down, ponder his plan, and enjoy a meal in peace whilst he felt excited at the thought of Nancy's success.

After an agreeable lunch Robert headed to Nancy's dressing room at the theatre.

"Oh Robert, why must you keep me guessing? Can't you just spill the beans about my next show? You know surprises aren't my thing," Nancy grumbled, seated in front of a mirror surrounded by bright lights. Feather boas adorned a nearby mannequin, and a velvet curtain closed to grant her privacy while she changed.

Nancy leaned closer to the mirror and applied her lipstick. She puckered her lips, ensuring an even spread of colour, then blew a playful kiss to her manager's reflection before putting the lid back on the lipstick.

"Because it keeps your excitement levels up, Nancy. The audience adore your enthusiasm on stage," Robert stood behind her and placed a tender kiss on her neck. He pulled away as Leo appeared through the curtains, deftly manoeuvring them to avoid getting tangled.

"Oh Leo, don't be shy. I'm sure you've seen that before. Is that the new costume?" Nancy excitedly snatched the dress from Leo's arm. She held it up, twirled in front of the mirror, and made the dress swish from side to side. Robert's fists clenched, and he crossed his arms, irritated by Leo's interruption.

"Do you want to try it on, Nancy? I've worked hard to make it perfect for your final performance," Leo offered, a hint of martyrdom in his voice.

Nancy grinned at Leo and led him behind a curtain to change into her new outfit.

Robert, visibly upset, raised his voice. "Do we have to do this now? I had plans to take Nancy out for dinner. I even made a reservation!" Robert drew in a slow, steady breath and felt his body tense.

Nancy and Leo shared concerned looks. Nancy could sense his disappointment and tried to ease the tension.

"Sorry, Leo. I should go. Maybe we can do it tomorrow? Come by at five, and we'll try it on then." Nancy handed the dress back to Leo. She emerged from behind the curtain and linked arms with Robert, leaving Leo with downcast eyes and a forced smile. *If Nancy keeps acting like this, she'll lose all her friends.*

"Where are you whisking me off to, Robert? I hope it's somewhere nice." Nancy's hand interlaced with his as they walked down the street. Theatre enthusiasts who had witnessed her performance couldn't help but stare.

"Let's celebrate your success at the Adelphi restaurant. It seems appropriate to dine there as it was the first place we went together."

When the couple arrived, Robert allowed Nancy to walk in front of him. "Can we have a bottle of your finest champagne, please?" Robert took the menu from the waiter and nodded. The waiter acknowledged the request and hurried off to retrieve the champagne and glasses.

"I'm starving. What are you having?" Nancy's eyes scanned the choices on the menu whilst unbeknown to her, something dropped in her glass.

Robert smiled at Nancy's straightforwardness, observing how the other diners began whispering amongst themselves and stealing glances at her.

"If I had ten pounds for every time someone looked at you, I'd be a rich man," Robert remarked, his tone tinged with a touch of envy. Nancy's little finger rested on the corner of her mouth as she looked up from the menu, deep in thought.

She scanned the restaurant, trying to comprehend Robert's comment. Whenever she caught someone's eye, she averted her gaze, feeling a touch embarrassed at being caught peeping at others. Her mother's voice echoed in her mind, "Stop being nosy, Nancy. Other people's business is none of your concern."

"And if I had a pound for every time someone looked at you, I'd be very wealthy." Nancy's sparkling eyes met the glances of fellow diners, and she swiftly looked away, unsure of the attention.

"They're not staring at me, Nancy. They're captivated by you. Can't you see their hunger for more? They want to know about your life and performances," Robert leaned back in his chair and observed the restaurant's curious onlookers. "Anyway, drink up, let's celebrate."

"Don't be silly. People couldn't care less about me," she said as she lifted her glass. As the rim of the crystal moved closer towards her lips, she noticed a dark shadow in the champagne. "What's that?" Nancy stuck a finger in her glass as her eyes widened with delight. "Robert? Surely—" Nancy's eyes glistened with emotion.

"It's true, my love." Robert stood up from his seat and got down on one knee in front of the performer.

"Yes! Yes! Robert, you don't even have to ask." Nancy held out her hand.

Robert retrieved a glistening ruby and diamond ring from the champagne glass. The deep ruby gem was shouldered by two diamonds and set in a gold band. The ring slipped seamlessly onto Nancy's wedding finger.

"Oh, Robert. It's beautiful. How did you know it would fit so well?"

"That is a secret that I will never reveal."

Nancy smiled at him as the whole restaurant looked on in admiration and celebration and clapped and cheered.

"A glass of champagne, madame?" The waiter topped up Nancy's glass and she held it in the air to chink against her fiancé's.

"I'm the happiest girl alive."

Robert noticed a gentleman rising from his table and heading their way. He had been keeping an eye on him throughout the evening, suspecting his intentions. The stranger's unwavering gaze had been fixed on Nancy all along.

"Excuse me, Miss Franklin. Could I trouble you for an autograph?" The man offered her a pen and a notebook. "I'm so sorry for intruding," the gentleman's cheeks flushed red and his wire-rimmed glasses nearly slipped from the end of his nose.

"At a time like this? How rude!" Robert declared.

Nancy, however, saw the stranger's sincere expression and felt a pang of empathy. "Of course, I'd be happy to. Is it for someone special?" Nancy inquired, her eyes meeting his as she took the pen and paper.

The man hesitated for a moment. "It's for my late wife. She watched you perform once at The Eagle Tavern, and the memory brought her joy until the day she passed."

Nancy's eyes sparkled with a mix of emotions, while Robert rolled his eyes impatiently.

"What's her name?" Nancy spoke softly, wanting to honour the memory of the man's beloved wife.

"Elspeth. She was a wonderful wife," the man had a touch of melancholy in his voice.

Handing the autographed paper back to him, Nancy offered her condolences. "I'm sorry for your loss. It is my pleasure to give this to you," she said, passing the signed piece of paper back to the grieving fan.

"You can leave us now you have what you want," Robert said, a cutting tone to his voice.

Nancy offered a sympathetic smile before the gentleman walked away leaving Nancy glaring at Robert. "There was no need for that, Robert. I was being kind. Can't you see the man has recently lost his wife?"

"You're too soft, Nancy."

"And you're too harsh, Robert. Now, are you going to refill my glass, or shall I beckon that charming waiter over there?" The temporary moment of celebration and happiness had passed. Nancy however playfully raised an eyebrow to diffuse Robert's mood. Robert obliged, pouring another glass of champagne, while Nancy surveyed the restaurant. Her gaze fell upon another gentleman making his way towards them, undeterred by Robert's cold stare.

"Excuse me, Miss Franklin. I apologise for the interruption," the man began, his eyes fixed on Nancy. Robert's arm tightened around her, drawing her closer as the man continued speaking.

"I couldn't help but notice your recent engagement. My congratulations. I'm aware your time at the Adelphi is concluding soon and wondered what plans you had in mind for the future," the man inquired, his tone filled with anticipation.

"Why is that any of your business? Nancy has a packed schedule, and we already know the next twelve months' shows. So, if you'll excuse us, we must be going," Robert interjected, his voice laced with a touch of hostility.

"But Miss Franklin, I can make you even richer than you are now. Richer than your wildest dreams," the man persisted, undeterred by Robert's cold reception.

Robert and Nancy paused in their tracks, their curiosity piqued. Nancy turned around, fixing her gaze on the gentleman before her.

"How do you propose to do that? I can't take on more shows than what's already planned for me," Nancy inquired, her interest piqued.

"I'm not suggesting full shows, Miss Franklin. Just the occasional song here and there. I believe you'll be in high demand," the man's eyes gleamed with excitement.

A quizzical smile formed on Nancy's lips, her eyebrows arched high. "That does sound intriguing. How much do you want?"

"We can discuss it later, Nancy. No need to decide now. Let's get going," Robert's arm pulled her in closer to his lean but strong body.

Robert and Nancy boarded their carriage, leaving the accomplished songwriter behind. As the carriage rolled on, Nancy couldn't help but worry if her happiness would last and whether Robert's jealousy would become unforgivable. He may have proposed, and for a moment, Nancy thought all her dreams had come true. But Robert's recent attitude left a lot to be desired.

Chapter Seven

Nancy glanced up at her father, her delicate white veil covering her pretty face. Her white silk gown cascaded to the floor, adorned with dainty pearls and intricate floral lace. Beneath the hemline, her white shoes peeked through, the dressmaker's deliberate design to ensure she wouldn't trip while walking down the aisle. Dolly, her younger sister, gazed on in admiration, silently hoping that she too would someday be married and look as beautiful as Nancy.

"You look wonderful, Nancy. I always knew you'd be the successful one," her father beamed, his voice filled with pride. "You have countless shows under your belt, a repertoire of songs, and people who love you. That's my girl."

Nancy's eyes met her father's, gratitude and love shining within them. She didn't want her younger sister to miss out on their father's compliments. "We're all successful in our own way, aren't we, pa?"

Nancy noticed her sister turning away, attempting to hide her embarrassment. She yearned to be as clever and accomplished as Nancy. Arthur caught on to Dolly's insecurities.

"Indeed, we are, Nancy. And Dolly here is doing well, helping others become more efficient at making the boxes. Isn't that right, Dolly?" Arthur's voice brimmed with warmth and encouragement.

Dolly's response was tinged with self-doubt. "Yes, but I'm not as glamorous or gregarious as Nancy."

Nancy's attempt to include her sister had fallen short. The young bride changed the subject, sensing the unease in the air.

"Has ma changed her mind about coming? I thought she would let go of her grudge against me for just one day."

Arthur mustered an upturned smile, although his furrowed brows and heavy sigh revealed his inner turmoil. He couldn't bring himself to lie.

"I'm sorry, Nancy. I tried to persuade her, but she wasn't having any of it."

"She takes the money I give every week, but on my wedding day, I'm not good enough for her." Nancy stole one last glance in the mirror, her right thumbnail removing a smudge of lipstick that had strayed beyond her lip line.

"It doesn't matter, Nancy. You look wonderful, and today will be the best day of your life." Arthur rested a hand on his daughter's shoulder.

"I hope so, pa. There are many more good days to come," Nancy said, her eyes sparkling with determination.

"Nancy, I'm sorry we have contributed little to the wedding. You know how things are these days," Arthur confessed, his voice filled with remorse.

Nancy took her father's hand, holding it gently. "It doesn't matter, it's more important that you're here with me."

Arthur hung his head in shame. He saw himself as the provider, even though there wasn't enough money for rent or bread. Nancy saved them from being cast out of their slum house and forced into the dreaded workhouse. The workhouses were gruelling, with long hours, strict discipline, and where no personal belongings were allowed. They were known for their clanking, deafening, industrial machines that could lead to injury or even death. Living in a slum house, despite going hungry was still preferable to being forever in a cruel, harsh, and unforgiving environment.

"Right, Nancy, Dolly, shall we go?" Arthur gestured, pulling his hands forward and sticking out his elbows so that his two daughters could link arms with him.

As they left the house, Nancy's brother Bill caught up with them, a mischievous grin on his face.

"Hey, Bill, don't you scrub up well! I've never seen you looking so posh," Nancy remarked, impressed.

"Anything for my big sister on her wedding day. But don't expect me to stay in these clothes all day. As soon as the wedding breakfast is over, I'll be changing into something more comfortable. I reckon I can make a fortune selling these clothes second hand," Bill looked down at his suit, stroking the material and flicking the buttons.

"Always the entrepreneur, Bill, aren't you?" Nancy pinched one of her brother's cheeks.

Bill smiled back, waiting for Nancy's long flowing satin train to pass before falling in line behind the rest of the family. Nancy and Arthur paused when they reached the front door, noticing the crowd that had gathered. Word had spread quickly—everyone wanted a glimpse of Nancy Franklin on her wedding day. Men, women, and children of all ages lined the streets, celebrating as if it were their own family member tying the knot.

"Oh, pa, look at all these people. Are they here for me?" Nancy's heart overflowed with joy.

"Well, I don't see anyone else getting married amidst this crowd, do you?" Arthur quipped, a twinkle in his eye.

Nancy beamed her brightest smile at her adoring fans, her arm waving high in the air as she stood on her tiptoes so those at the back could catch a glimpse. The performer spun around, captivating the crowd, while her father and siblings patiently waited for her finale. As she took her final steps, the footman opened the carriage door, and all four of them climbed inside. Nancy was the first, ensuring she lifted her white silk dress to preserve its pristine condition, with Dolly's helping hand. She cherished the gown and wanted to keep it in perfect condition for eternity. Arthur, Dolly, and Bill followed suit, taking their seats beside or opposite Nancy. The carriage door closed, and the horses trotted along the cobbled streets, making their way to the church.

Nancy kept waving as the crowds thinned, allowing the horses to speed up and get the bride to the church on time. She felt an overwhelming happiness, but a part of her wished her ma were waiting there. Their relationship had been fraught with difficulties. Memories of slaps and harsh words still haunted Nancy, making her cringe inwardly. Yet, Jenny was her ma, and that special bond couldn't be broken, no matter how hard they tried.

The carriage arrived at the church's lychgate amidst joyous bell ringing on a warm summer day. Nancy despised the heat, so she had insisted on a wedding date that wouldn't be too warm. The sun always made her perspire and dampened her shirt collar. But Nancy wanted her wedding in the summer—it was the least she could ask for, considering she was financing the extravagant affair. The night they discussed it, Nancy had indulged in one too many drinks, and her impatience grew. She couldn't comprehend why her sudden assertiveness had relegated Robert's choices to second place.

Champagne and liqueurs flowed until their disagreement over the wedding date escalated into a loud argument. Mrs Jackson, their neighbour, banged her broom handle against her ceiling three times, desperate to silence their late-night quarrel. Fair enough, it was past midnight, and they both knew Mrs Jackson retired early. When they moved into the flat above, she had kindly informed them of her early bedtime and requested no noise after ten o'clock.

The next morning, Nancy chose to remain silent about the events of the previous night. Robert attempted to make amends by taking her out for lunch and shopping at the new department store in Knightsbridge. It worked, to some extent, in distracting Nancy from the hurtful words and abuse she endured. Yet, beneath her outward facade, the pain still festered, fuelled by Robert's cruelty.

Now, on her wedding day, Nancy's main concern was hiding her growing bump beneath her wedding dress. Tabloids exposing her unwed pregnancy was her worst fear. It could cost her fans, her performances—everything she had worked so hard for. Announcing the child's arrival would be a daunting task. It wouldn't take much for her adoring public to piece together the timeline, realising she had conceived before her wedding. But that was a bridge to cross when it arrived.

Her mind filled with these conflicting thoughts, Nancy's attention was drawn to her mother standing at the end of the front pew. Making her way towards her groom, Nancy's heart swelled with love and anticipation. Her father proudly presented her to Robert, their eyes locking in a moment of promise. Arthur had no inkling of what had transpired that fateful night three months prior. If he had known, Robert would not be standing at the altar awaiting his bride; instead, he would be struggling to walk at all.

The organist's fingers played the final notes, and the foot on the pedal offered a gentle conclusion to the music as Nancy prepared to marry her dashing fiancé.

"You look beautiful, Nancy," Robert gave his bride to be a wide grin as Arthur stepped back to take a seat.

Dolly and Bill slipped into their places behind the front row, sitting beside Aunt Margaret and Uncle Harold. Watching their sister, they saw her take her place beside her fiancé at the altar.

With heartfelt vows and promises of unwavering support, the couple sealed their love in the eyes of the law. But their commitment would be shattered within a year, leaving Nancy with neither husband nor child.

Throughout the ceremony, Robert couldn't tear his eyes away from Nancy. He held her hand after sliding the ring onto her finger, his smile a testament to his affection. Since that night three months ago, he knew he had crossed a line. Nancy became withdrawn and was no longer the gregarious performer with the same forceful control she once possessed. Today, however, they put their differences aside, exiting the church as man and wife. Nancy's mother caught her attention, and Nancy approached her, enveloping her in a warm embrace.

"I know you didn't want to come, but I'm so glad you're here. It means the world to me," Nancy expressed, her voice filled with sincerity.

Jenny accepted the gesture, her bitterness set aside. "I wouldn't have missed it, Nancy. My oldest daughter getting married. I had to witness the spectacle for myself. Even if it's just an extravagant affair that will vanish as quickly as it appeared."

Jenny's biting words pricked Nancy's heart, but she bit her tongue, refusing to let any retaliation slip past her lips. In that moment, Nancy vowed to treat her own child differently when it arrived, to break the cycle of resentment and jealousy.

"It's my day, and I'll celebrate my wedding however I choose. I'll see you back at the house," Nancy mustered a smile despite the hurt.

Jenny raised an eyebrow and turned her gaze away, concealing her mixed emotions. It was money she had never possessed, and jealousy clouded her pride. Despite Nancy sending money home every week since she ran away from the slum house, it was never enough to garner her mother's approval or quell the envy that gnawed at her.

"Nancy, shall we go?" Robert showed for Nancy to link arms with him as they made their way to the waiting carriage. The crowd erupted in applause and cheers for the newly married couple.

"Did you see my mother, Robert? I can't believe she came. I'm so happy," Nancy's voice was laced with a mixture of joy and apprehension and anger at her ma's recent exchange of cutting words.

"I didn't notice, to be honest. My eyes were only on you, my beautiful wife," Robert nuzzled into Nancy's neck.

Nancy couldn't help but feel a tinge of unease, aware of the surrounding crowd. "Stop it, Robert. The crowd can see us."

"So what? You're my wife now, and I can do as I please," Robert's tone of voice was strained and he gripped his wife's knee tightly.

"Cut it out, Robert," Nancy gave a bark of laughter and pulled away from him, attempting to diffuse the tension in the air.

Undeterred, Robert continued his behaviour until they reached their home. Fortunately, the journey was short. He gallantly stepped out of the carriage and helped his wife descend the steps.

"Wait here for a moment," he said with a mischievous glint in his eyes.

Nancy furrowed her brows, puzzled. But before she could question him, Robert scooped her up into his arms, carrying her over the threshold of their home. The crowd erupted in cheers and applause, witnessing the symbolic act of crossing into their new life together. Nancy stood by his side just inside the doorway, ready to greet their guests, her heart filled with love and anticipation.

Nancy and Robert graciously exchanged greetings with each guest as they entered their home. As they finished, Nancy's gaze was drawn back to her mother, who seemed increasingly unwell. Worried, Nancy approached her, her heart heavy with concern.

"Are you alright, ma? You don't look well at all," Nancy inquired, her voice laced with worry.

"I'm fine, Nancy. I couldn't miss the chance to witness my oldest daughter's wedding." Jenny's voice was strained.

Nancy couldn't tear her eyes away from her mother, her anxiety growing. After the last guests arrived for drinks, she pulled Jenny aside.

"Can I tell you something, ma?" Nancy glanced around, ensuring no one eavesdropped on their conversation. "I want to tell you in private," Nancy guided her ma to the study.

Jenny followed her daughter without hesitation, sensing the gravity of what Nancy was about to reveal.

"Ma, something has been weighing on my mind. I know you won't be pleased, but I feel I need to tell you before anyone else finds out,"

Nancy began, her voice filled with a mix of trepidation and determination.

Jenny gazed at her daughter and then down at Nancy's belly. A moment of understanding passed between them.

"You're with child, aren't you?" Jenny's words cut through the air, her tone a mix of resignation and concern.

Nancy was momentarily stunned, her own fears and secrets laid bare. "How did you know?"

"A mother always knows when her daughter carries life within her. I take it this was not a choice you willingly made?"

Nancy's eyes welled up with tears, and her voice trembled as she confessed, "I'm so sorry, but I didn't have a choice."

Jenny's gaze softened, and she reached out to hold Nancy's hand. "I knew it. That man does not deserve to be your husband."

Suddenly, Jenny clutched her chest, her hand attempting to quell the pain that surged within her.

"Ma, Ma! Are you alright?" Nancy's voice rose in panic. She called for help, hoping someone would come to their aid.

Arthur, hearing his daughter's distress, rushed to their side. Robert followed suit, curious about the commotion. The two men stopped suddenly, almost crashing into each other, when they saw Jenny on the floor, clutching her chest.

"Please, pa! Help her!" Nancy knelt by her mother's side, her wedding dress forming a circle of white around her as she leaned over Jenny's body.

Arthur shook his wife's shoulder, desperately hoping for a response. But there was none. He placed his fingers on her wrist, searching for a pulse, but found none. Tenderly, he turned her onto her side and held her hand, while Robert rushed to the telephone to call the doctor. When he returned, his face etched with worry, it was too late.

Jenny Franklin had already been claimed by the angels, her final breath extinguished.

Nancy sat by her mother's side, her father's arm wrapped around her trembling shoulders as she wept.

"This is the worst day ever. Just when I thought Ma, and I were reconciling, she's gone," her lips trembled and her heart felt heavy with grief.

Overhearing her words, Robert's face twisted with anger, his expensive wedding now marred by tragedy. Nancy sought solace in her father's lap, while her husband stood by, consumed by frustration at the ruined celebration.

Tragedy cut short a day meant for joy. The natural order of events had been upended, leaving a bitter taste in their mouths.

Chapter Eight

Nancy sat in the office of the funeral director, her figure draped in a long, jet-black silk dress. The vibrant white wedding gown that once symbolised joy and celebration had been replaced, swallowed by the heavy cloak of mourning. The recent death of her mother had cast a bleak shadow over her newfound happiness, and whispers of speculation about the cause of her mother's untimely demise permeated the air.

"It was the shock of her daughter's wealthy suitor..."

"Her daughter, the cause of her own mother's demise..."

Only three days after her mother's funeral, a newspaper headline shattered Nancy's heart.

"NANCY'S MOTHER DIES AT WEDDING AFTER HEARING HER DAUGHTER CONCEIVED OUT OF WEDLOCK!"

Nancy had wept for a full twenty-four hours while her new husband, Robert, watched helplessly. Curled up in bed, she shut herself away from the world, refusing to see her father and Leo, her closest confidantes.

Between her sobs, dark thoughts gnawed at Nancy's mind. "Robert, I'm so ashamed. The entire world knows our child was conceived before our wedding. I hope you're proud of what you did to me that night!"

In her search for blame, she found an easy target in her husband, but this only strained their relationship further. Since discovering her pregnancy, Nancy had kept Robert at arm's length, and he grew increasingly agitated. The previous night, in a fit of frustration, he had visited a brothel to seek solace, returning home intoxicated at two in the morning. Desperate for attention, he had attempted to wake Nancy, but she kept her eyes closed, refusing to engage in yet another argument.

Now physically, and emotionally exhausted, sleep-deprived Nancy found herself burdened with arranging her mother's funeral.

"Don't worry, pa. I'll take care of the expenses," Nancy assured him, sitting by her side in the funeral director's office. She had resolved to deal with Robert later, as her mother's funeral took precedence.

"Miss—sorry, Mrs Wheeler," the funeral director began, peering over his gold wire-rimmed glasses.

"It's still Nancy Franklin. I may be married now, as the papers have no doubt informed you, but my name is and always will be Nancy

Franklin. That's how people know me," Nancy refusing to abandon her identity.

The funeral director cleared his throat, unsure of how to respond to her statement. "Sorry, Miss Franklin. The funeral will cost seventeen pounds and three shillings and the cortege will travel through Whitechapel, up to the Strand, and back—"

He glanced down at his notes, searching for the details.

"—to the church where Sid and Amelia are buried. Are you sure you wouldn't prefer a proper burial with a headstone? Do we need the cortege to travel to the Strand?"

"My mother would want to be buried with Sid and Amelia, wouldn't she, pa?" Nancy turned to her father, who nodded, his face stained with tears, a tattered handkerchief clutched in his trembling hand.

"The Strand is non-negotiable. She never had the chance to see me perform, so it's only right that she sees the theatre where I rose to fame."

Mr Wigton, the funeral director, regarded Nancy with growing understanding. "I appreciate your reasons, Miss Franklin. However, if you keep the cortege within Whitechapel, you could save at least five pounds."

"It's not about saving money, Mr Wigton. We want to give her the best funeral we can, don't we, pa?" Nancy's gaze was fixed on her father, who nodded again, his eyes filled with grief and gratitude for his daughter's dedication.

"My ma deserves nothing but the very best."

Nancy couldn't help but feel the weight of loss and regret pressing down upon her.

"Very well. In that case, we'll bring your mother's body to the house tomorrow, and the funeral will be in three days' time. Questions?" Mr

Wigton looked back down at his notebook to make sure everything had been covered.

"No, thank you. I hope you'll do my mother justice with the service. No funeral is too grand for her," Nancy stood up from her seat, glancing at her frail father, who remained seated beside her, his spirit broken. Together, they made their way out of Mr Wigton's office, leaving the lanky funeral director standing alone.

The journey back home was sombre, the carriage carrying Nancy and her father was silent and both were enveloped in their own thoughts. Nancy felt a sense of relief that there were no fans waiting outside the funeral home, eager to exploit her grief. However, the cracks that had already formed in her marriage lingered in her mind, threatening to overshadow her mourning. She couldn't help but wonder how she and Robert would bring a child into a world when they seemed incapable of caring for themselves, let alone each other.

Nancy rested her hand on her growing belly and pleaded with her unborn child. She hoped against hope that it couldn't sense the anxieties and strains that plagued her relationship with Robert. With five months remaining until the baby's arrival, she resolved to protect it from her own worries, vowing to create a haven of love and stability.

"Miss Franklin, we've arrived," the footman declared as the carriage stopped in front of Nancy's house. After the wedding and her mother's passing, Nancy had invited her father and siblings to stay with her and Robert. Despite Robert's displeasure, Nancy insisted, asserting her ownership of the house, which she had purchased with her earnings from her performances.

"Nancy, we've just got married. Do they have to stay?" Robert protested.

"Yes, they do. This week, my mother died. Right now, I feel torn between you and my family," Nancy asserted, her voice firm. The strained dynamic with her husband compelled her to take a stand.

"Well, if you're torn between me and them, maybe you made the wrong decision marrying me. I don't want them staying here!" Robert's frustration seeped through his words.

Later that night, as Robert's attempts to bend Nancy to his will failed, he disappeared into the night while Nancy cried herself to sleep, unaware that her money was funding his indulgences in brothels and liquor.

The following day, Nancy and her father arrived home in the carriage she had arranged. Arthur had insisted the night before that he wanted to go back to the marital home, just for a while. Nancy was relieved to find no unwanted fans lurking outside. She helped her father inside, supporting him under one elbow with both hands.

"Can I help you, Miss Franklin?" George, the footman, offered, glancing at Arthur's frail mobility.

"No, thank you, George. I'll take it from here. You can finish early and go see your family. You never know what's around the corner; they could be gone in an instant," Nancy's voice was filled with a mixture of gratitude and weariness.

"Very well, thank you," George tipped his hat as a gesture of appreciation. He turned and left Nancy and her father to find solace in their grief.

Chapter Nine

━━━✦━━━

Did everything go well?" Robert's voice greeted Nancy as she stepped into the house.

Nancy took a moment to assess his tone, searching for genuine concern beneath his words. "Yes, as well as can be expected. Pa was naturally upset, but that's to be expected."

"It'll take time for him to heal, no need to rush. Dolly and Bill are upstairs in the spare room. They've had some lunch, and I thought I'd start a fire. It got a bit chilly this afternoon," Robert's words were laced with a hint of tenderness.

Nancy glanced at her husband, unsure of his true intentions. "Thank you, and I hope you don't mind, but they're bringing ma here tomorrow. How about the drawing-room for her? We can each spend time with her before the funeral. What do you think?"

"I think it's a fine idea. When is the funeral?" Robert's voice softened as he focused on Nancy's needs.

"Two days from now. You'll be there, won't you?" Nancy was desperate for his reassurance.

"Yes, of course, I'll be there, Nancy. You and the young one's need me now, so consider it done," Robert opened his arms, ready to embrace his wife. Nancy leaned into him, feeling the warmth of his touch and hoping against hope that his sensitivity would endure. She wanted nothing more than to shield her baby from her own fears and uncertainties, to create a stable and loving environment. Nancy relished in his embrace and prayed it would last.

After dinner, Nancy, Arthur, and Robert sat in the living room, seeking solace in the crackling warmth of the fire. Dolly and Bill had retired to bed, leaving the three of them to confront their grief together. Nancy nestled against her husband on the sofa, seeking comfort in his presence, while Arthur sat alone in a wingback chair, lost in his own thoughts.

Nancy couldn't help but notice the way Robert's hand reached for the decanter, pouring himself another drink. She considered requesting one for herself, but hesitated slightly, aware of the new life growing within her.

"I'll have one of those too, please," Nancy's gaze fixed on the flickering flames.

"I don't think that's wise, do you? There are two of you to consider now, not just yourself," Robert responded, concern lacing his words.

"Oh, come on, Robert, a small one won't hurt. It might even do the baby some good—kill any germs, you know. I don't want our child to have a short life like Amelia or Sid," Nancy remarked absentmindedly, her thoughts clouded by grief and weariness.

Startled by her words, Robert grabbed her by the hair, yanking her head back. Nancy winced in pain, tears welling up in her eyes. *I knew his kindness wouldn't last.*

"I said no!" Robert's voice came out harsh and forceful.

"Ouch, Robert! You're hurting me!" Nancy cried out, her voice filled with both pain and indignation.

"Do as I say," he pushed her face. Nancy curled her feet underneath her, tears streaming down her face. She knew this kind of coercive love wasn't what she wanted.

Robert stormed off to bed, clutching a generous portion of brandy in his hand, leaving Nancy alone and shaken. Meanwhile, Arthur, though appearing asleep, had heard every word and witnessed the mistreatment of his beloved daughter. *I should have listened to Leo. I need to do something about this*, he resolved silently, before sleep finally claimed him, transporting him to dreams of happier days with his wife, who was now lying cold on a slab in Wilton's Chapel of Rest.

Chapter Ten

※

The day of Jenny Franklin's funeral arrived, leaving no expense spared. The London General Mourning Warehouse had supplied the necessary attire—millinery, dresses, cloaks, hats, gloves, and mantels—for the grieving family, ensuring that everything was ready well in advance.

"I don't want to wear this blasted suit, Nancy. Look at it! Can't I just wear my regular clothes?" Bill, Nancy's young brother, slouched in front of the mirror, his shoulders drooping.

"No, you can't. Today, you'll show your mother some respect. She did everything for you, so the least you can do is look presentable.

We're all going through a tough time, Bill, and wearing a suit is the least you can do," Nancy responded firmly, her voice carrying a mix of sorrow and determination.

Bill let out a sigh and rolled his eyes, the weight of grief pressing down upon his young shoulders. At fourteen, he had been forced to mature beyond his years, grappling with the loss of three family members.

"Come on, Bill, let's go," Nancy wrapped her arm around her younger brother's shoulder and planted a kiss on the top of his head.

"Ger off," he shrugged her away with a feigned nonchalance, refusing to accept his sister's sign of affection.

"You're never too old for a kiss from your big sister, Bill. You should know that by now," Nancy playfully shoved him, though he resisted her efforts. A knock on the bedroom door interrupted their playful interaction, and their father, Arthur, entered the room.

"How do I look, Nancy? Will this do? I hope Jenny would be proud of us all today," Arthur's voice was tinged with vulnerability.

Nancy saw her father standing there, consumed by sorrow, a mere fragment of the man he used to be. He had lost the strength to hold the family together in their grief, leaving Nancy to shoulder the responsibility.

"Oh, Father, you look wonderful—dapper, even. Ma would be proud. She never saw you in such a fine suit, but she'll be watching from above."

"Thank you, Nancy. I don't know what I would've done without you this past week. It's been so hard, you know. Her passing was so sudden, and I didn't know how to cope," Arthur admitted, his voice trembling with raw emotion.

"Come here," Nancy took her father's arm and led him downstairs, where Dolly, Bill, and Robert awaited.

Descending the stairs, a knock at the door interrupted the solemn moment. Robert, ever the dutiful host, opened the door, revealing a figure holding the largest bouquet he had ever seen. The vibrant colours overwhelmed his eyes, while the fragrant scent filled the hallway, causing him to sneeze three times. The delivery person quickly averted their gaze, covering their nose and mouth with their elbow to protect themselves from any impending disease.

"Delivery for Miss Franklin, sir," the delivery man handed the flowers to Robert before swiftly departing.

"I wish you would go by your married name, Nancy. Otherwise, what's the point of getting married?"

"But everyone knows me as Nancy Franklin. It's my stage name. And I didn't marry you for your name; I married you for love," Nancy's voice carried a mixture of weariness and frustration. She reached up, pinching Robert's cheek playfully, attempting to defuse any potential argument that might arise.

"Considering you insist you have no admirers, you seem to be receiving anonymous gifts quite frequently," Robert remarked, his suspicion evident in his voice.

"I've told you, Robert, I have no idea who sent me that gift last week, and I certainly don't know who sent these flowers today," Nancy stood, picking at her fingernails. She placed the note accompanying the flowers on the hall table, trying to put the mysterious gesture out of her mind.

Nancy swallowed her rising anxiety, resenting the flowers for casting doubt and fear into her husband's mind. She disliked how they sowed seeds of suspicion and threatened the fragile peace between them. The vibrant, fragrant blooms may have symbolised the warm summer, but they brought complications she could do without. Speaking in a low, strained tone, she addressed Robert's concerns.

"We'll discuss this later," Robert's grip on Nancy's wrist tightened momentarily.

That was the thing about Robert—Nancy never knew where she stood with him. She took a step back, freeing herself from his grasp, and placed the flowers on the hall table, refusing to let them further taint the sombre atmosphere.

"Who was at the door, love?"

"Oh, no one, pa. Just a mistake," Nancy caught Robert's gaze. Her eyes pleaded with him to drop the subject.

Together, they continued their solemn march, making their way outside to the carriages, waiting to transport them to the graveyard. The glass carriage holding Jenny's coffin was adorned with delicate pink and white flowers, a poignant tribute to a woman who had meant so much to them all.

Nancy and her siblings stood nearby, watching as their father approached the hearse. Arthur gently caressed the cold, smooth surface of the coffin, seeking some connection with his departed wife, his fingers lingering as he whispered his love and devotion. Nancy's eyes were momentarily blinded by the flashing bulbs of hidden photographers among the crowd, their presence a reminder of the intrusion into their private grief.

As they entered the church behind the coffin, Nancy, Robert, and her siblings passed rows of mourners filling the wooden pews. The overflowing church was evidence of Jenny's impact on others. They took their seats on the front row, their bodies weighed down by sorrow, their hearts heavy with loss. Robert reached for Nancy's hand, but she withdrew, clasping her hands in front of her, finding solace in her own strength.

The vicar's prayers echoed softly throughout the church, mingling with the sombre tones of the organ. Yet, the words seemed distant, barely audible over the heartbreaking sobs of Arthur and Dolly. All four remaining family members linked arms, finding strength and support in each other's presence as the service carried on. Robert stood unnoticed, his attempts to reconnect with his wife met with indifference.

The sound of dirt being shovelled into a grave filled the air as the service ended. Jenny's body was laid to rest beside Sid and Amelia, a final reunion in the embrace of the earth. Her family stood together, tears mingling with memories, contemplating a future without her.

Meanwhile, Nancy's attention was momentarily drawn to a familiar face among the mourners. She stared, her gaze fixed on the man standing among the crowd. Percy Hartman. The memory of their encounter in the Adelphi Theatre restaurant a few months ago flooded her mind. She couldn't fathom why he would be present at her mother's funeral. Her curiosity piqued, she resolved to unravel the mystery surrounding his intentions.

They mourned together and said goodbye to the woman who had been the heart of their family. Nancy's emotions swirled within her, a potent mix of sorrow, uncertainty, and the weight of the challenges she faced. As they filed out of the church, she clung to her family, finding solace in their presence, even as questions about Percy Hartman danced at the edges of her thoughts.

CHAPTER ELEVEN

※

Robert tore down the remnants of mourning draped over the house. Black crepe, like a growing mountain, piled up next to the front doorway, casting a shadow over the lives. The night air hung heavy in Robert's presence and Nancy trailed behind him, desperation etched on her face, pleading for more time to grieve.

"It's not time, Robert," she implored, her voice a fragile tremor. "Only a few weeks have passed. Please, I'm still grieving."

But he brushed her aside, callous and cold, rejecting her touch with each attempt. In a moment of fury, he pushed her with a force that sent her sprawling onto the polished floor. Heavily pregnant, Nancy instinctively protected her precious belly and prayed that her child remained unharmed. Her fingers brushed against her rounded bump, seeking solace in the tiny kicks that reminded her of life's resilience.

Robert's gaze met hers, and for a fleeting second, she hoped for empathy, a hand extended in compassion. But he had other priorities. His voice thundered through the house, demanding that every clock be set ticking again, as if the relentless march of time could heal their wounds.

"You have a show in five days, Nancy. We can't delay any longer," he barked, his tone devoid of understanding. "You'll lose fans, money, and they'll move on to another star. Pull yourself together!"

Nancy's shoulders sagged and tears mingled with the gentle caress of her unborn child. She sat on the floor, her legs splayed apart, whilst she pleaded with her husband. "I can't do the show, Robert. I simply can't. My audience doesn't want to see me like this. They want the real Nancy, the one who brings joy and distraction."

Robert knelt before her, their proximity uncomfortably close, Robert's chest nearly brushed against her swollen belly. His breath, heavy with the stench of alcohol, assaulted her senses, and she instinctively turned her head away.

"You'd better find that happy-go-lucky woman, hadn't you?" His voice dripped with menace. "Or I'll tarnish your reputation, ensuring you never step on another stage again."

The spittle from his words splashed upon her skin, his threats like venom in the air. He stood abruptly and made his way towards the stairs, halted only by an unexpected knock at the door, which shattered their tense standoff.

"For heaven's sake, can't we have a moment's peace?" he grumbled, yanking open the door.

A gentleman peered around the frame, his eyes searching for a glimpse of Nancy. "I was wondering if I could have a word with Miss Franklin?"

Nancy's heart skipped a beat, anxiety clawing at her as she braced herself for Robert's reaction. In Robert's eyes, any male voice or stranger held the potential for a jealous rage.

"Hold on a minute. I know you, don't I?" Robert's brow furrowed as he strained to recall their previous encounter. "You're the bloke from the restaurant, trying to con my wife out of money!"

Percy Hartman, undeterred by Robert's aggression, peeked around the door's edge, his gaze widening upon seeing Nancy. Robert moved closer, shielding her from view.

"Is everything alright? Does she need help to get up?" Percy's concern filled the air.

"What do you want? We're busy, and it's late!" Robert's hostility loomed.

"I was wondering if Miss Franklin had reconsidered my offer to write songs for her," Percy persisted. "I could make her even more famous, you know."

Nancy, her eyes still damp, desperately hoped Hartman wouldn't stir up more trouble. "No, thank you. I'm not interested. Now, please leave us alone."

Bristling with possessiveness, Robert stepped closer to Percy, his gaze fixed and unblinking. "I'm her husband, understand?"

With a shove, Robert sent Percy stumbling backward, his hat rolling onto the street. As a passing carriage crushed the trilby and splashed muddy water on Percy, Nancy couldn't help but wish ill upon Robert. *What a horrid, wretched man! I hope he chokes on his supper and releases me from his vicious torment.*

Nancy supported her belly with a hand as she stood up. She leaned against the hallway table adorned with her mother's photographs, still turned away as a symbol of unresolved grief.

"I didn't know you were in contact with Percy Hartman?" Suspicion tainted Robert's words.

"I'm not," Nancy cautiously kept her responses brief to avoid triggering Robert's wrath. She silently prayed that her controlled demeanour would prevent an outburst.

"Is that so? Then how does he know where you live?"

"It's not difficult, is it? The whole world knows where I live. There have been photographers outside the door since I moved in. Weddings, funerals, sold-out shows—they all attract attention. He wouldn't have had to put in much effort to find me."

A realisation dawned on Robert, his eyes narrowing with suspicion. "I get it now."

"What do you mean?" Nancy's voice trembled.

"The flowers and the wedding gift. They were both from him, weren't they?"

"I have no idea who they were from. I've told you that already. Now, why don't we sit down and have a nice supper? I'm starving, and our little one needs nourishment, too."

Robert's gaze lingered on her for a moment, and Nancy dared to hope for a moment of peace, a glimmer of the man she had fallen in love with. But his response shattered her optimism.

"Forget it. I'm going out. Get yourself cleaned up. I'll see you later. Remember, five days, and I want you show-ready."

He snatched his jacket from the hook and stormed out, leaving Nancy to pick up the pieces. Mr Hartman, lurking in the shadows, waited for Robert to disappear down the street. Tonight, it seemed fortune smiled upon him. He adjusted his jacket collar, adopting a determined stance, and followed Robert's retreating figure.

Robert's return came in the early hours of the morning, reeking of perfume, cigarettes, and liquor. Nancy had tried to cry herself to sleep, seeking solace in slumber, but her tears had proved futile. Instead, she lay awake, listening to the familiar sequence of sounds—a slammed front door and his heavy, stumbling footsteps on the stairs. Her body braced itself for what would come next.

In the dim light, Robert undressed and slipped under the covers, his scent a reminder of his absence. Nancy's heart clenched with a mixture of fear and resignation. As his weight settled beside her, she whispered a silent prayer, hoping for an uneventful night.

Chapter Twelve

As Nancy concluded her final song, the audience erupted into a tempestuous applause, rising to their feet in a wave of adoration. Cheers filled the air, blending with declarations of love and thunderous requests for more. Nancy curtsied gracefully, blowing kisses to the hundreds of people who had eagerly awaited her return to the stage because she had doubted it was the right time. The hundreds of people in the audience gave her a sense of hope, a sense of purpose, and an escape from her wretched husband.

After one more encore, Nancy stepped off the stage, her eyes catching sight of Robert seated in the balcony. Flanked by two women who shamelessly caressed his shoulders, he puffed on his cigarette, basking in their attention. *How could he be so audacious with our child coming soon?* Nancy fixed him with a cold, hard stare, her heart heavy with disappointment.

"Here, Leo, lend me a hand with this costume. It's too tight with the little one inside," Nancy sought assistance from her loyal friend.

Leo diligently unfastened the twenty buttons at the back and untied the ribbon around her waist. Each discarded piece of clothing found a place on the freestanding mirror in her dressing room. As Nancy slipped out of the costume, Leo's gaze fell upon a large, ugly bruise on her shoulder, eliciting a wince when his finger grazed it.

"Ouch! I bumped into the dresser in the drawing-room a few days ago. It's turning yellow now, though, so it'll clear up soon," Nancy hoped she'd managed to fool her dearest friend. She didn't want Leo to know the truth.

Leo met her gaze squarely, his eyes brimming with concern. "Nancy, you can't fool me. I know what's going on."

"I don't have a clue what you're on about," Nancy said, walking over to the dressing table to remove the remnants of lipstick from her lips.

"You do know, Nancy. How long will this continue? How long before he puts an end to you and kills your unborn child too?" Leo's voice carried a mix of determination and worry.

"Who? Robert? You must be joking. He wouldn't harm me!"

Leo stepped closer, placing his hands gently on her shoulders. "Perhaps not directly, but I see through it, Nancy. One day, you'll reach your limit and either fight back or lose yourself entirely."

"Nonsense! How dare you speak ill of him? He loves me, he does!"

"That's not love, Nancy, and you know it. Love doesn't leave bruises or revel in the company of other women while his wife toils away."

Leo's grip tightened, his hands a comforting anchor. "I love you, Nancy. I'm your best friend, looking out for you."

"I know you are. I'll be fine, truly I will."

"What's the matter now?"

Unbeknownst to both Nancy and Leo, Robert had sneaked into the dressing room. He leaned against the doorframe, a cigarette dangling from his fingers. Nancy couldn't help but notice the lipstick smeared across his neck.

"I'm talking about the baby and taking care of myself," her voice tinged with weariness.

"You'll be fine. The more its mother performs, the more likely the child will become a star," Robert turned his gaze away from his wife.

Nancy averted her eyes, feeling the weight of Leo's hands upon her shoulders, restraining him from confronting the vile man. She forced a smile, placing her hands atop Leo's. "I'll be fine, I promise," she whispered.

"If you have something to say, at least speak up so everyone can hear," Robert interjected, his presence cutting through the room.

Nancy didn't know what to say.

"As Nancy said, she was talking about the baby, and I have a few personal problems too, she was helping me," Leo hoped he sounded convincing.

Robert looked at them both. Satisfied that Nancy wasn't blackening his name any further, he changed the subject. "Well, hurry up then. Let's go for dinner, I'm sure Leo can finish off on his own, can't you?"

Nancy didn't give Leo a chance to respond. "Why, what's the rush, dear husband? Can't we have a night off? I'm exhausted and in need of rest," Nancy pleaded, desperation seeping into her voice.

"No, I want to go out. Come on," Robert reached for his wife's hand and tightened his grasp around her slender fingers.

Left behind to tidy up, Leo watched them depart, his concern for Nancy etched deeply on his face.

Nancy knew better than to defy her despicable husband's demands. She allowed his hand to envelop hers, and they exited through the stage door, cameras flashing and fans clamouring for autographs.

"Nancy, could you sign this for me?"

"Wait, Nancy, let me capture a picture. Perfect, just like that."

Fans and photographers pursued Nancy relentlessly for a piece of her. Robert pushed his way through the crowd, clearing a path for them. Just as they thought they left everyone behind, a man appeared.

"Not you again? Get out of our way!" Robert barked, his frustration apparent.

He shoved Percy Hartman, but this time, Percy managed to keep his footing. The crowd surged forward, eager to witness the unfolding drama. Flashes from the cameras illuminated the scuffle, magnifying the tension for all to see.

"Are you sure you don't want me to write those songs for you, Nancy? I'd do you proud, you know!" Percy taunted.

"No, thanks. I'm good. I don't need any more songs," she regretted the words as soon as they had left her mouth. She glanced over her shoulder at Percy as she walked away, Robert's grip tightening on her hand at the sound of Percy's voice and invitation.

"Are you absolutely sure? I wouldn't want to resort to spilling your secrets to the press just to get you to reconsider," Percy raised his voice for all to hear.

Robert abruptly halted, spinning around on his heels. His face contorted with anger. "How dare you? Get out of my sight!"

"Or what? You'll take your anger out on Nancy again? Or if that doesn't satisfy your anger, may you could go and visit the brothel again like you did the other night?" Percy's voice thundered, shocking the crowd into silence as they strained to hear more revelations.

"I said, get out of my sight, Hartman!" Robert's fury was palpable.

The tension crackled in the air as the two men stared at each other, their eyes locked in a battle of wills. The crowd held their breath, anticipating the eruption that loomed on the edge of violence.

Without warning, Robert lunged at Percy, his fist colliding with Percy's right cheekbone. The impact echoed through the night and it sent shockwaves of pain through both of them. Nancy gasped, her hands flying to her face as the camera shutters clicked, capturing the violent clash.

Percy, fuelled by a surge of righteous indignation, retaliated with a powerful blow of his own. His fist connected with Robert's jaw, sending him staggering backward. Blood trickled from Robert's split lip, staining his chin.

"You don't deserve a woman like Nancy. You're a disgrace!" Percy's voice boomed through the air, carrying the weight of his disdain.

Enraged, Robert charged forward, attempting to regain his balance. The crowd gasped, their murmurs blending with the camera flashes that illuminated the chaotic scene. Robert, unable to contain his fury, lunged forward, grappling Percy by the waist. He exerted all his strength, pushing him back into the circle of spectators that had formed around them.

A ring of onlookers encircled the grappling duo, their collective breaths held in anticipation. The atmosphere crackled with tension as the fight intensified, both men unleashing a torrent of punches, fuelled by their simmering animosity. Blood sprayed through the air, mingling with sweat and grime, as the two combatants traded blow after punishing blow.

The cobbled ground beneath their feet became a battleground, a canvas upon which their anger played out. The spectators watched in awe and horror, their eyes widening with each devastating strike. Camera shutters clicked incessantly, capturing the raw and brutal scene, freezing the violence in time.

Nancy stood at the periphery, her heart pounding in her chest, tears streaming down her face. "Robert! Robert, stop!" Nancy's voice was laced with desperation. Her pleas echoed through the chaos, a haunting melody that reached the ears of all who listened.

But the frenzy of the brawl drowned out her cries, the combatants too consumed by their rage to hear reason. The clash spilled beyond the confined alleyway, onto the bustling main street, drawing the attention of passersby who had emerged from the theatre's entrance. A growing crowd, their eyes widened with shock and morbid fascination, encircled the fighters, their whispers merging into a cacophony of gossip and disbelief.

Sensing the crowd's voracious hunger for spectacle, photographers jostled and clamoured for the best vantage points, their cameras poised to capture every blood-soaked moment. The flashes of light illuminated the fight, lending an ethereal quality to the chaos, freezing the fighters in a series of dramatic tableaux.

As the combatants rolled and grappled on the unforgiving ground, their faces contorted with rage and exhaustion, Nancy's heart shattered into a thousand pieces. She clung to Leo, her fingers digging into his arm, a lifeline amidst the whirlwind of violence. Her anguished sobs mingled with the gasps and murmurs of the crowd, her voice a piercing lamentation for the man she had once loved.

Suddenly, Robert, in his blind fury, saw an opening and made a reckless dash for escape, leaving his pregnant wife behind to confront the aftermath. Oblivious to the world around him, his eyes fixed on the path ahead, he sprinted away from the crowds and Percy Hartman.

But in a cruel twist of fate, Robert failed to notice the oncoming omnibus hurtling towards him. The thunder of hooves and screeching of wheels sliced through the air, mingling with the horrified screams of onlookers. Time slowed, each passing second an eternity, as the crowd filled carriage collided with his body. He was sent hurtling through the air, a rag doll caught in the grip of destiny's wrath. His descent ended abruptly as his head collided with the street cobbles, blood spilling forth in a thick, dark stream.

Nancy's world shattered in that split second, her screams swallowed by the chaotic symphony of hooves, wheels, and shouts from onlookers. She rushed to her fallen husband, her trembling hands cradling his broken body as tears mingled with the thick pool of blood beneath him. Onlookers stood frozen, their faces a mask of shock and disbelief, as the haunting reality of the moment sank in.

Chapter Thirteen

It was a difficult task on a dreary and rainy evening. Moving an anonymous body was challenging enough, but when it was Robert Wheeler, the married husband of the country's most famous entertainer, things were even worse. The unwanted crowd obstructed the two men as they tried to lift Robert onto the stretcher. At one point, a young boy with tattered clothes and dirty cheeks attempted to steal Robert's wallet from his jacket.

"Hey, what do you think you're doing?"

Fortunately, the boy stumbled and dropped the wallet, which landed a few feet away. The undertaker ran forward and picked it up from the ground. The boy laughed and ran into the night.

Rain poured down that night, its heavy drops pelting the streetlights and cascading onto the cobblestone road below. Rainwater carried away Robert's congealed blood into the sewers. As Nancy knelt on the wet pavement, cradling her husband's head against her unborn child, she knew he was gone. She rocked him back and forth, calling out his name with desperation, but his eyes remained lifeless.

Percy Hartman stood in shock, looking down at Nancy. He never intended for Robert to die. He had no desire to fight. Nancy's husband may have been prone to disagreements and throwing his weight around, but fighting and vengeance were not Percy's style. Yet, once he was attacked, he had no choice but to defend himself. He couldn't believe the level of violence Robert was capable of, and he wondered what Nancy had endured during their marriage.

The crowd lingered, watching Nancy's grief-stricken display. Photographers vied for the best angle in the crowd in the pursuit of the best photograph. Meanwhile, Nancy stood on the rain-soaked street, crying out for her lost love. She recalled the night she had resolved to leave him. But now, with that decision snatched away, she realised how deeply she loved him despite his despicable and violent behaviour.

Once the undertakers had completed their work, Leo gently detached Nancy from Robert's lifeless body and guided her back home. He assisted her in undressing, akin to undressing her after a show, and tucked her into bed, pulling the covers up to her chin. She trembled from the cold and shock, so her loyal friend fetched her a hot water bottle, a cup of tea, and additional blankets to keep her warm. When her heavy eyes could no longer stay open, she drifted into sleep, and Leo quietly left the room.

Arthur and his children were awakened by a loud thud on the front door an hour later. Their evening had so far been uneventful. They had decided not to attend Nancy's first show in a while, as she had urged them to rest after the emotional toll of Jenny's loss. Arthur had spent the evening as usual, searching the streets for matchbox orders, and returned home to a meal of chicken and vegetable stew prepared by Dolly. After supper, they all sat on their beds, reminiscing about the family they once had.

"Who is knocking at the door at this ungodly hour? Arthur shook his head, sighed, and swung his legs over the bed as the knocking grew louder.

"Alright, alright, I'm coming!"

He swiftly pulled open the door, revealing a drenched and sobbing Leo on the doorstep.

"Leo! What's happened? It's not Nancy, is it?"

Leo nodded, then shook his head, unsure of his response because of the mixed nature of the news. Dolly and Bill adjusted to the darkness and eavesdropped on the conversation at the door.

"I need my coat. Just wait a moment."

Arthur closed the door to fetch his coat from the rusty nail behind it. He slung it over his arm and walked over to Dolly's bed, a luxury furnished by Nancy.

"Dolly, Dolly, there's been an accident. I must go see Nancy. Can you stay and look after your brother? Don't worry!"

Arthur didn't wait for a response, knowing that his youngest daughter would take care of Bill while he was away. Hastening down the worn concrete steps, he struggled to keep up with Leo as they made their way through the muddy and filthy courtyard. They emerged through the decrepit wooden gates onto the silent street.

"Are you alright, love? Fancy a bit of entertainment tonight?"

A nearby prostitute took a drag from her cigarette and blew smoke rings at Leo and Arthur, attempting to catch their attention as they rushed past her, ignoring her advances.

"Hey, you can't ignore me like that! I deserve an answer, at least!"

The prostitute tutted and moved along in the opposite direction, disappointed that her spot had attracted no business that night.

"Leo, what's happened?" Arthur quickened his pace to keep up with the family friend.

The men hurried down the street. They both caught their breath whilst trying to speak at the same time. Despite the chilly weather, Leo's back was drenched with sweat.

"It was dreadful, Arthur. Nancy was visited by Percy Hartman after the show, which Robert didn't like. They exchanged punches, and Percy called him a disgrace, shouting that he didn't deserve a woman like Nancy!"

"Well, that's true and not surprising. I've been meaning to have a word with him ever since Jenny passed. I've disliked how he's treated my daughter from the start. He spoke ill of her, unaware that I was listening, even on the night before the funeral."

"Yes, well, it's too late now. Robert's dead!"

Leo hastened, not bothering to check if Arthur was keeping up with him.

"He's dead?" Arthur said, stopping in his tracks, his face frozen with shock. "Surely not?"

"Yes, Arthur. I'm sorry. Robert's gone."

Arthur stood with his hands on his hips wondering what to say. Should he speak the truth?

"Well—well, I'm kind of—kind of glad. He didn't deserve my daughter. Not my Nancy." Arthur closed his eyes and shook his head. "Oh, dear God, Nancy. Her unborn child. What will happen now?"

"I don't know. All I know is that she will need us and we need to get to her. This loss and her mother's death are now Nancy's burden. She has upcoming shows and will have to raise their child alone. I just don't know how she'll manage, do you?"

Arthur shook his head, uncertain how Nancy would survive this ordeal. He feared she would turn to liquor to cope, his stomach nervous as he thought of the consequences.

Chapter Fourteen

A week later, Nancy descended the steps from her front door, stepping onto the street teeming with crowds and photographers. "They must be here for more trouble," she thought, weary of the damage caused by their intrusive headlines. She hadn't yet recovered from the previous onslaught.

"NANCY'S HUSBAND DIES AFTER A STREET BRAWL AND SCANDALOUS RUMOURS OF INFIDELITY!"
"NANCY'S NEWLY WEDDED HUSBAND KILLED IN A FIGHT LEAVING HER SHOWS IN JEOPARDY!"

"NANCY FRANKLIN FACES SINGLE MOTHERHOOD AFTER HER UNFAITHFUL HUSBAND'S DEMISE!"

After reading four different newspapers, all filled with lies, Leo and Arthur banned any further publications from entering the house.

Each line Nancy read pierced her heart, reducing her to tears and making her feel utterly hopeless. She should have known better than to read what the papers said. *Come on, Nancy, you can do this.*

Arthur placed a fatherly arm around her, guiding her down the steps while her siblings supported her on the other side. For once, Nancy touched the glass of the hearse with feeble hands, contemplating the bleak future ahead now that her husband was gone.

The flashes of photographers' cameras seemed incessant. The crowd fell silent, a low murmur and whispers only heard as she climbed into the Brougham carriage. She couldn't discern whether their presence stemmed from sympathy or mere nosiness, drawn to the unfolding drama.

The funeral director directed the horse-drawn hearse towards St. Mary's Church. Nancy wondered how many mourners would attend the service. Robert had no known family, and his only friends were the women he encountered during his nightly escapades away from Nancy. As the carriage moved on, Leo and her family sitting beside her, it became clear that every time she entered a church, her loved ones diminished in number.

"Look at all these people. I hope they don't expect me to speak." Thankfully, her black veil concealed the sorrow and tears on her face.

"They don't expect you to do anything, Nancy. They're here to pay their respects."

She nodded briefly, acknowledging her friend's reassurance that she could retreat from the world's gaze until she felt ready to face her fans again.

As the hearse and carriage came to a stop outside the church, six hired men lifted the coffin from its glass enclosure. Leo, Arthur, and Bill had no desire to carry him to his final resting place after the way he had treated their beloved Nancy.

They followed the coffin into the church. Nancy couldn't believe the amount of mourners outside the church, who had come to pay their respects. Or were they there to stare out of curiosity? "Leo, who are all these people? I didn't invite them. In fact, the only ones invited are you lot. So who are they?"

"Perhaps they're old friends and acquaintances. They probably won't stay for the service."

Leo held Nancy's hand and stroked the palm with his thumb, trying to offer some comfort in the face of the unexpected crowd. Together, they entered the church and took their places on the front pew. She didn't recognise many people in the congregation and the grieving widow felt her chest tightening at the thought of nosy gossip mongers imposing on her sorrow. She felt herself on the verge of collapse under the weight of her sorrow. Her hand gripped Leo's, whilst her father rushed to support her from the other side.

The vicar acknowledged the mourners before commencing the prayers. The church was almost empty. As the vicar began, Nancy glanced left and right, then looked over her shoulder, hoping to recognise a familiar face. She only knew one person in the congregation, the man at the back. Nancy didn't know how to react to seeing Percy there. What he had said on that fateful night had been true, but he had continued the fight that led to her husband's death, leaving her unborn child fatherless.

She nudged Leo and flicked her head towards the back of the church. Leo turned around. He was shocked by Percy's presence at the funeral of the man he had caused to be hit by an omnibus.

"What is he doing here?" Leo shook his head in the direction of the alleged songwriter.

"I don't know, but he must have some persistent reason," Nancy rolled her eyes and then gazed at the hymn sheet as the music started.

The congregation stood and began singing "Abide With Me," led by the vicar.

'The darkness deepens; Lord, with me abide.
When other helpers fail and comforts flee.
Help of the helpless, O abide with me.'

For once, Nancy couldn't bring herself to sing. She stood with her head bowed, gazing at the floor, rubbing her aching pregnant belly. A sudden fear gripped her as she realised she hadn't felt the baby move. Thoughts raced through her mind, struggling to recall the last time she had felt a kick or a flutter within her limited space. Panic surged within her; grief had consumed her to the point of neglecting the tiny life growing inside her. "Oh no, my baby hasn't moved for an entire day!"

"What did you say, Nancy?" Leo said.

She realised she had spoken her thoughts aloud, unintentionally revealing them to the entire pew. "I said my baby hasn't moved for a whole day."

"Don't worry, Nancy. It's just sleeping. Your mother experienced that with you. Let the vicar finish, then we can take you home and get you some help." Arthur held her hand, attempting to reassure her that her baby was fine. But fate had other plans.

Nancy cried out in pain, her knees buckling as her father and Leo tried to support her. She was about to collapse on the floor and gasped in horror. "Oh No! No! No! No!" Tears streamed down her face, mingling with saliva filled with bubbles.

Her family and Leo followed her gaze, paralysed with shock. The vicar halted his sermon, and the church fell into a heavy silence.

Chapter Fifteen

"Please, please help me." Nancy lay on the cold stone floor gripping Leo and Arthur's hands.

The priest called short the service and asked everyone to clear the church. Nancy deserved the privacy but the onlookers couldn't move. All frozen with worry and shock, they were eventually ushered out slowly.

"Leo, we need a doctor, please. Can you hurry?"

"I'm a doctor, I can help!" There was a cry from the back of the church. A gentleman rushed forward and quickly kneeled down to the expectant mother. Taking her pulse and feeling her forehead he shook his head. "How pregnant is she?"

"Erm—erm—Leo? Do you know, I've forgotten," Arthur said.

Nancy's best friend shook his head in disbelief. "I did know. I knew exactly, but it's gone. It must be the shock, I think she may be six months—something like that." Leo watched the doctor move towards Nancy's pelvis then his gaze shifted towards his friend's pale and sallow face. Nancy's eyes had gently closed as a pool of blood formed on the floor.

Suddenly, Nancy took a deep breath in and was alert as she cried out in pain. "I need to push!"

"Nancy, Nancy, listen to me. I want you to follow what I'm going to say," the doctor said with concern in his voice.

"But it's too soon, it's way too soon. It will never survive," Nancy looked up at the doctor in horror.

"Nancy, my main concern is you. We have to help you, and for you to survive you are going to have to push."

Nancy nodded whilst her hands shook. And with every ounce of breath and energy she had, she pushed with all her might.

Chapter Sixteen

No one knew where to look as they witnessed Nancy Franklin lose her child. There was no way the baby would have survived with the amount of blood loss present on the church floor.

The vicar made the sign of the cross above her and prayed for God's protection. Arthur preserved his daughter's dignity by covering her with coat and both he and Leo held her hands and stroked her forehead. Nancy would need all the strength and prayers they could muster.

"It's likely because of the tight costumes and recent loss of her mother and husband." The doctor looked up and raised his eyebrows.

"With all the stress she's put herself under, it's not surprising," the doctor explained to Leo and Arthur.

Nancy's two siblings had been sent away to witness the burial of their brother-in-law. Dolly and Bill had followed the vicar leading the coffin out of the church, accompanied by a small congregation.

The vicar rested a comforting hand on their trembling shoulders. "Dear, oh dear, poor children. They've witnessed some awful things in their young lives."

Arthur Franklin's appearance had aged twenty years in just a couple of months. He had endured his own grief and that of his children. He watched on as his family attend another funeral, and it weighed heavily on his heart. He knelt down beside his daughter and grasped Nancy's hand.

"Don't worry, Nancy. I promise you'll be alright," Arthur reassured her.

"Yeah, Nancy, we're here with you now." Leo unpinned and removed Nancy's black hat and short veil, then stroked her damp hair. He wondered how much more sorrow his best friend could bear.

"Turn those things off, will you? Who is ringing the bells?" the doctor barked, his orders echoing throughout the church.

Leo stood up and hurried to the back of the church, where a bell ringer was pulling the heavy bell-rope. He addressed the bell ringer, attempting to remain polite despite the urgency of the situation.

"Excuse me, could you please stop? The doctor can't concentrate with all that noise going on."

The rope slipped from the bell ringer's grasp, soaring above his head as he declared victory over the bells' resounding toll. Upon watching the scene unfold before him, his face turned as pale as a ghost. Realising the gravity of the situation, Leo rushed to his aid, guiding him out of the church and into the fresh air.

As the bell ringer stumbled away, Leo noticed a growing crowd of people outside, their curiosity piqued by the commotion. Among them was a journalist who had been sent to report on Robert's funeral. He anticipated that this unexpected turn of events would secure him the promotion he had long awaited. Nancy's loyal friend wondered what scandalous story would grace tomorrow's front pages. He knew that Nancy didn't need any more negative publicity, especially after postponing her shows because of her husband's sudden death. She questioned whether Nancy would even be fit enough to return to the stage.

"It looks like the baby is about to arrive. Please give the woman some space!" The doctor took charge of the situation, guiding Nancy through the painful process of giving birth, while Arthur and Leo held her hands. Their faces filled with silent screams as Nancy squeezed their hands with all her might.

"Push again, Nancy. I know it's difficult, but you must try to concentrate," the doctor urged.

"I just want the baby to be alive!" Nancy cried out.

The doctor remained silent. As the child emerged, its frail and premature form became apparent. Its tiny lips and hands were tinged with blue, and its eyelids remained closed. The doctor slowly closed his eyes and shook his head. Tears welled up Arthur and Leo's eyes. They looked away briefly, trying to not let their sadness show.

Nancy was only six months pregnant and knew she was delivering a lifeless child. Overwhelmed by shock, she turned her face to the side and vomited on the stone floor after pushing. She lacked the strength to wipe her mouth, let alone stay awake long enough to find out the gender of her baby.

Arthur decided that he would break the news to her later.

"We need to get this woman to a hospital. Does anyone have the funds to pay for an ambulance?" the doctor glanced at Arthur and Leo.

Arthur felt ashamed that he couldn't afford an ambulance for his daughter. He looked at Leo, pleading for help.

"Yes, I do," Leo spoke up, determined to ensure Nancy received the care she urgently needed.

While they awaited the ambulance, the vicar returned to the church. He blessed both Nancy and the lifeless child, offering a moment of solace before the undertakers arrived to take the baby away.

Leo left Arthur to follow his daughter to the hospital, unaware that Percy Hartman was watching the drama unfold from the sidelines. He was entangled in the latest chapter of Nancy Franklin's tumultuous life, unsure of how it would impact his chances with her. The unexpected events in the church forced him to consider his next move.

Meanwhile, Leo approached Dolly and Bill, wrapping his arm around them both for support.

"Come on, you two. Let's go home," Leo suggested, knowing that fresh air would help clear their heads. Weighed down with grief, they began the long one-hour walk back to Whitechapel, braving the drizzle outside. As they trudged along, they couldn't help but wonder when—or if—they would see their beloved Nancy again.

Chapter Seventeen

Arthur sat alone in the hospital corridor, his mind consumed by worry. Hours felt like an eternity as he anxiously waited for news about Nancy. His shoulder was shaken gently, jolting him from his thoughts.

"Mr Franklin, she's stable now. You can go in and see her. But remember, only thirty minutes. She needs as much rest as possible," the nurse's voice was laced with compassion.

Arthur stood up slowly, using the back of the chair for support. He cautiously approached Nancy's bed, passing rows of iron beds occupied by other ailing patients. Some looked at him with tired eyes, while others lay motionless, their faces hidden beneath the covers. The late summer sunlight filtered through the large windows, casting a gentle glow on the wilting flowers by the bedsides, providing a fleeting burst of colour in the otherwise sombre ward.

Arthur reached Nancy's bedside and settled into the wooden chair placed there by the nurse, anticipating his arrival. For a few minutes, he gazed at his daughter, his heart heavy with concern for her well-being.

"Oh, Nancy, my love. Your mother is watching over you. Please stay strong," Arthur's voice was filled with tenderness. He held her hand and stroked it, trying his best to convey his unwavering support. Arthur fought back tears, determined to show strength and courage in front of his daughter. Yet, the sight of Nancy lying motionless overwhelmed him.

"Please, Nancy, pull through." Arthur sank to his knees and rested his head on the edge of the bed. His tears dampening the cotton sheets as he sobbed uncontrollably.

It was time for Arthur to leave. Nancy needed rest. "Mr Franklin, you have to go now, your daughter needs to recuperate."

Arthur lifted his head out of his hands and looked at the nurse. His eyes were red, his cheeks mottled.

"Take heart, Mr Franklin. We're doing everything we can for her. She's a fighter," the nurse reassured him.

Three days passed, each moment filled with anxiety and uncertainty. Percy Hartman, eager to know Nancy's condition, bought a newspaper from a street vendor near Trafalgar Square. The headline on the front page captured the tragedy that had befallen Nancy Franklin.

"NANCY FRANKLIN CLOSE TO DEATH AFTER TRAGIC STILLBIRTH AT HUSBAND'S FUNERAL!"

The headline screamed, its callousness striking Percy's heart.

Disgusted by the insensitive reporting, Percy extinguished his cigarette and discarded the paper in a nearby bin. He walked toward St Thomas' Hospital, determined to see Nancy for himself. Percy approached the nurse stationed at the entrance, putting on a concerned expression.

"Excuse me, I'm her half-brother. I've travelled all the way from Scotland to see her. Could you please let me in for a few moments? I promise I won't overstay my welcome."

The nurse hesitated for a moment, considering the flowers that covered Percy's arm. "Alright, just thirty minutes. She needs her rest, and she's still a bit drowsy."

Percy felt a wave of relief wash over him as he walked towards Nancy's room. He hoped that she wouldn't scream or reject him. Instead, he held onto one vision—that Nancy would recover and allow him to compose songs for her, and perhaps, even marry him. Percy had loved her from afar for years and refused to let this chance slip away.

Chapter Eighteen

Leo and Arthur flanked Nancy, each holding one of her arms, as they guided her up the stone steps to her black front door. The warmth of the September sun lifted Nancy's spirits, a welcome change after spending four long weeks in the women's ward at St. Thomas' hospital. In those early days, she hadn't been aware of any visitors. Only her closest loved ones appeared sporadically, offering solace and holding her hand as she recovered from the traumatic loss of her child at her late husband's funeral.

Upon waking in her hospital bed, weak from the horrific blood loss and the death of her baby, Nancy was surprised by the abundance of flowers adorning her bedside. The flowers were shared with other patients in the ward to brighten their lives. Nancy managed only a faint smile and slow, blinking eyes in response, a silent agreement with the sister's actions.

"Even your half-brother from Scotland has come to visit you, Nancy," the sister revealed, her voice full of admiration. "He's staying in London for as long as you're here in the hospital. It's a lovely gesture, don't you think?"

Nancy's grogginess from her awakening that morning didn't hinder her realisation that she had never had a half-brother. She couldn't fathom who the visitor might be. Could it be Leo, perhaps? Maybe he had pretended to be her half-brother to stay by her side and hold her hand while she recovered. The sister leaned in, speaking softly into Nancy's ear to ensure no one else could hear.

"You're a very fortunate girl, you know. We usually only permit male relatives, but seeing how concerned and distressed Leo was about your condition, we allowed him to visit you a few times as well."

This revelation only deepened Nancy's confusion. In the absence of Leo pretending to be her half-brother, who else could it be? She remained silent, not voicing her thoughts to the sister, pondering the mystery whilst contemplating her recovery and her eventual return to the stage.

Four weeks later, Nancy was finally strong enough to leave the hospital. Leo and Arthur arrived to collect her, assisting her on her journey back home. However, a few days before her departure, Percy Hartman once again appeared at her bedside, bearing yet another bouquet. With no space left beside Nancy's bed, the grateful sister accepted the flowers and placed them near a woman in the ward. She had never had any visitors or flowers of her own. Percy nodded his approval and took a seat next to Nancy, patiently waiting for her to awaken.

The moment Nancy opened her eyes, she knew Percy was the man who had fabricated their relationship so he could see her. She wasted no time in expressing her anger.

"You've got some nerve, haven't ya? Visiting me here? If it wasn't for you, Robert would still be alive. And I dare say my child would be too. How dare you show your face at a time like this? Who do you think you are?"

Percy settled into the iron chair beside her bed, staring at the floor and nervously biting his fingernails. He knew Nancy had every right to be angry, considering the circumstances of Robert's death. But he believed Robert deserved his fate, and it was his mission to make Nancy see that he was the one who would care for her, protecting and cherishing her for the rest of her life. However, he realised it wasn't the right time to reveal such feelings. Courting her so soon after her husband's death would appear insensitive and might push her away.

"Nancy, I'm so sorry. I didn't want a fight with Robert. All I want is to write songs for you, songs that would propel your fame. But for some reason, your late husband was opposed to the idea. And I wonder why that might be. If he hadn't attacked me that night outside the stage door, the accident would never have happened. I had no choice but to defend myself.

Nancy shifted in her bed, unsure if she wanted to hear more from him. She sensed his discomfort and allowed him to continue.

"I want to make it clear that I never pushed Robert into the path of that tram. He recklessly ran across the road without looking, and tragedy struck. Before the accident, he was even willing to abandon you and deal with the consequences alone. He didn't care about you, Nancy."

THE STARLET SLUM GIRL

The truth of Percy's words struck Nancy hard. She had always felt second best in Robert's eyes, emotionally neglected and pushed aside. Despite giving him everything he desired, including the money to visit brothels, she had been trapped in a relationship filled with abuse and torment. She remained silent, allowing Percy to pour out his thoughts.

"I believe a man should never abuse a woman, physically or verbally. Yet whenever I saw Robert with you, Nancy Franklin seemed to fade away. He claimed to have made you famous, to have given you the break you needed, but in reality, he acted like a narcissist, taking everything away from you once he had what he wanted. And it certainly wasn't love; it was your money." Percy shifted uncomfortably in his seat.

Nancy looked at him and blinked slowly, turning her head away from words she would rather not hear.

"Your fans could see the truth, especially with the headlines in the news. They sympathised with you, but what could they do? The only way to support you was to keep attending your shows, hoping that, after your mother's passing, you would return swiftly."

Nancy's chin dropped to her chest as she quietly sniffled. She didn't want Percy to see her vulnerability, but his words touched her deeply.

"I saw you perform that night when Robert died. It was a relief to see you on stage, but I could tell you weren't yourself. You weren't ready to return, and I could sense that Robert had forced you into it."

Nancy couldn't deny any of Percy's words or allegations against her late husband. Each one was painfully true. But how could she trust Percy, a man she hardly knew, so soon after being betrayed by her late husband? She was exhausted from her ordeal, lacking the energy for a lengthy conversation with the man who sat by her bedside.

"I can't deny what you're saying, Percy, but what do you expect me to do? Are you suggesting that you whisk me away from here? That you'll take me somewhere safe, marry me, and promise never to leave? Is that what you want? I'm not sure I can trust anyone after Robert. He met me one night after my performance, promising me the world. For a few months, I felt like a queen. But then, as soon as he had what he wanted, his attitude changed. The abuse began. How do I know you won't be like him?"

Nancy looked at Percy. His eyes shimmered in the sunlight with unshed tears. Percy's voice trembled as he replied, his vulnerability laid bare. "I would never harm you, Nancy, not physically or verbally. It's not in my blood. It happened to my ma and I don't ever want to see that again."

Nancy gasped, her hand flying to her mouth. "Oh, Percy, what happened? Why would your Pa do such a thing?"

Percy slowly looked up and met Nancy's eyes. "It wasn't my pa, Nancy."

Nancy frowned at Percy, waiting for him to continue.

"I don't remember much, only that the man she worked for was horrible. She was in his office one day and I heard her cry for help. Everyone else ignored it. Well, they had to if they didn't want the same treatment."

"Percy, please, you don't have to tell me," Nancy reached for his hand.

Percy raised his eyebrows and sighed deeply. "My pa had a suspicion that something wasn't right. So he went to meet her from work one day with Grace. He caught them both leaving the mill then—then this wretched man forced himself on my ma. Pa saw it all."

Nancy started to cry, her mouth hung open, not knowing what to say.

"My pa was furious as you can imagine. He went to protect my ma and pushed her to one side whilst he showed Mr Wilson what it was like to be beaten up."

"How do you know?"

"Because I ran out of the workhouse to catch up with ma and Grace. When I saw what was happening though, I crouched down behind a bush so no one could see me."

"What happened after that?"

"Mr Wilson hit my pa too hard. It was enough to kill him. I saw my pa collapse against the wall and he didn't wake up. Then I remember Mr Wilson being furious. He looked at ma and Grace and started walking after them. My ma had no choice. She let out this piercing scream and ran with Grace."

"Oh, Percy, this is terrible." Nancy's tears began to flow, the memories of her own mother's tragic fate resurfacing, and reminding her of her powerlessness on her wedding day. The memories haunted her still, and Percy's words made them feel as fresh as yesterday. "What happened to your pa?"

Percy shrugged his shoulders. "I don't know. I assumed he was dead. He didn't flinch after Mr Wilson went after my ma and Grace. And I was so scared I ran back to the workhouse, I collapsed in a dark corner and sobbed. I never saw any of my family again."

Nancy couldn't help but feel inspired and touched by Percy's life story. Deep inside, she sensed that perhaps he was a man she could trust. She needed to regain her confidence in relationships, and perhaps starting with him, once she had fully recovered, was the right thing to do.

"I'm sorry you had to endure such a tragedy. I know the pain of abuse all too well. But can I ask, what happened to your sister and ma?"

"I don't know. I never heard from them. I guess they were so scared they dare not return home. I remember Mr Wilson walking into the mill the next morning, but I never saw ma and Grace again. That was me in the workhouse until I was old enough to leave."

With slow, deliberate movements, Nancy extended her hand towards Percy. Her fingers brushed against the white cotton sheet until they found his clenched hands, resting silently at her side.

"Percy, perhaps when I'm discharged from here, we can meet and talk further."

"I would be delighted, Nancy. Truly delighted. And I hope that one day, you might find it in your heart to forgive me for that dreadful night."

"Oh, Percy, there's nothing to forgive. I saw Robert dart across the street, oblivious to the danger, and collide with that omnibus. You were nowhere near him. He has only himself to blame. In fact, considering how he treated me as his wife, I believe I would have continued living a life of torment had he survived. So, I am grateful to you instead."

Percy smiled at Nancy, rising from his chair while still holding her hand.

"I look forward to seeing you when you're discharged, Nancy, and I hope that one day we can be more than friends."

Nancy nodded and watched her new friend stand up, walk between the rows of iron beds, and exit the ward. Nancy was left to ponder his words.

Chapter Nineteen

Nancy had been at home for a few days giving her time to think about the conversation with Percy in the hospital, and recover from the death of her husband. The remorse and sadness she had felt in the church was no longer there. Just a realisation that since his death, her life was about to begin again. Unlike her mother's death, she had refused to cover the mirrors, turn the photographs around, or stop the clocks.

Arthur threw back the curtains in his daughter's bedroom. "Well, Nancy, what can I fetch you? A cup of hot, sweet tea and a cold meat sandwich, perhaps? How about a slice of fruit cake too? That hospital food couldn't have been anything decent. You must be famished!" Arthur suggested, eager to cater to Nancy's needs.

Normally, Nancy would protest, mindful of maintaining her figure. But now, she understood the importance of accepting every offered kindness as a blessing.

"That sounds wonderful, pa. Did you make the cake yourself?"

"No, it was Dolly who made it. And speaking of Dolly, your siblings can't wait to see you. I've arranged for them to visit this evening. Is that alright with you?"

"I'm looking forward to seeing them, pa," Nancy had a glimmer of anticipation in her eyes.

As Arthur went to fetch Nancy's lunch, Leo turned to Nancy, a genuine smile on his face.

"You must be overjoyed to be home, Nancy. I was so worried about you these past four weeks. I can't imagine life without my best friend by my side."

"Come here, you sentimental old thing," Nancy beckoned him closer with open arms. As he embraced her, she whispered, "I was never going to let go. I have so much more to accomplish, so many performances and shows waiting for me. As soon as I'm well, I'll be back at the Adelphi Theatre, entertaining all those patient, kind fans who've been waiting for my return."

"You're an inspiration, Nancy." Leo was about to leave the room when they heard a knock at the door, muffled voices coming from downstairs. They exchanged glances, wondering who the visitors could be.

Nancy knew instantly that Percy Hartman had come calling.

"Who is it, Nancy? Do you know?" Leo had concern etched on his face.

"Yes, it's Percy."

THE STARLET SLUM GIRL

"Alright, I'll go and see what he wants. You're not up for visitors yet, are you?"

"I am for Percy. Please ask pa to let him come upstairs. He visited me in the hospital and brought me so many flowers. He's truly a decent gentleman, and there's nothing I'd love more than to see him and show him how far I've come since we last met."

Nancy pulled the bed covers up to her bosom, her eyes fixed on the door as Percy entered her room, a bouquet of the most beautiful flowers Nancy had ever seen in his hand.

"I thought you might be missing some flowers, Nancy. This time, you can keep these all to yourself."

"They're beautiful, Percy. Would you mind putting them on my dressing table by the window? Leo will get me a vase."

After placing the flowers down, Percy noticed a few photographs of Robert still scattered around the room.

"How are you, Nancy? Recovering well, I hope? You look better than the last time I saw you," Percy looked around, observing the room's surroundings.

Percy's concern touched Nancy's heart. Perhaps, together, they could find their way back to the stage, helping one another in their respective journeys.

"I was thinking about you before I left the hospital. I wondered if you would be willing to help me get back on stage. Would you, Percy?"

Percy looked at Nancy, his eyes filled with a mix of anticipation and excitement. He took a deep breath before responding, his voice filled with determination.

Chapter Twenty

"I'm so nervous, Percy. I hope they'll give me a warm welcome." Nancy fidgeted in front of the mirror in her dressing room. Small lights and scattered costumes filled the room, leaving little space. She smoothed out the final creases in her outfit, twirling around to ensure she looked her best from every angle.

Leo buttoned up the tiny peach silk buttons at the back of her corset, tying a pastel pink satin ribbon into a large bow at the top of her skirt. He adorned her headdress with light grey feathers, making sure her tightly pinned curls would hold throughout the performance.

"This costume has been my biggest challenge, Nancy. I know how important this opening night was for you, I wanted it to be perfect. Trust me, you'll be brilliant," Leo assured her, offering a warm smile.

Nancy couldn't help but feel a bit uneasy, recalling how Robert had reacted with jealousy to Leo's compliments in the past, trying to sabotage their friendship.

"Even if the fans don't give you the reaction you're hoping for, remember that I am your biggest fan. You'll always have a special place in my heart," Leo noticed Nancy's unease.

She glanced at Percy, waiting for his response to Leo's kind words, still wary from the previous experiences with her husband.

"There's nothing for you to worry about when you're with me. I've said it before, and I'll say it again—I would never say a bad word about you or harm you in any way. So, please, don't fret," Percy assured her, his words bringing a sense of relief to Nancy. Her tense shoulders relaxed, and her racing heart began to calm. With hope in her eyes, she sighed and smiled at Percy. However, the pre-performance nerves still churned in her belly, causing her stomach to flip countless times over.

"You'll do just fine, Nancy. We've all been eagerly awaiting this night, and the audience will adore you. Have you seen the headlines in the papers these past few days?" Leo's excitement was evident.

Nancy had seen the headlines, nervously flipping through the newspapers to read what the unscrupulous journalists had written about her. But she needn't have worried. The articles were filled with nothing but praise from the eager and enthusiastic writers. It was a stark contrast to the previous headlines when she miscarried at her husband's funeral.

"Can you hear that? The fans are clapping and shouting your name, awaiting your entrance on stage. They're hungry for you. It's time to gather your nerves, my love, because they're waiting for you, and you're going to be extraordinary."

Nancy took a deep breath, the sound of the cheering fans echoing in her mind. She knew that despite her absence, her loyal fans had remained steadfast, awaiting her return. The three months she had spent recovering from her ordeal had been filled with doubt and fear. Nancy questioned whether she would perform again and if her fans would remain loyal.

Luckily, her father, siblings, and Leo had taken good care of her during her recovery. Percy would sometimes visit with sugared almonds or a slice of fruit cake. They would spend afternoons talking, sharing stories, and shedding tears over the traumas they had faced in their lives.

As Nancy closed her eyes, she could still vividly picture those moments spent with Percy. She would sit in one of the wingback chairs in her bedroom, donning a dressing gown over her nightclothes, while Percy listened attentively. He never spoke unless she finished recounting the hardships she had endured. In return, she would lend him her ear, wiping away tears as he shared the painful memories of losing touch with his family as a young boy.

Those afternoons had always ended with Nancy falling asleep in front of the fire, wrapped in a thick woollen blanket as Percy quietly left the room, ensuring he didn't disturb her slumber.

The opening night performance ended with the audience on their feet, applauding and demanding encores, showering the stage with single roses. Nancy stood there, taking in the magnificent sight—the joy of being back on stage, the overwhelming support from her adoring fans. She graciously curtsied, a radiant smile on her face. Her eyes shimmered in the spotlight's warm glow, her wispy head feathers dancing in the air.

THE STARLET SLUM GIRL

The crowd continued to chant her name until she gestured subtly, urging them to quiet down. It was time to sing. Nancy needn't have worried about losing fans during her absence. Three months had passed, and she feared the worst. But she had missed being on that stage, pouring her heart out through song, dance, and performance. And now, she had made her triumphant return.

As the curtains were drawn, revealing Nancy standing alone in the centre of the stage, the applause roared to life. She felt the surge of energy from the crowd, the love and adoration washing over her. Her long-awaited moment had arrived.

The performance was flawless, each note and movement executed with precision. From the balcony, Percy watched the captivated audience through his binoculars with sheer joy on his face. This was where her heart belonged, as he had predicted.

As she walked offstage, waving and blowing kisses to the crowd, Percy and Leo rushed to greet her. Their smiles matched her own, filled with pride and elation.

"That was wonderful, Nancy! I knew you had it in you. Through those tiny binoculars, I could see the happiness in your eyes. This is your calling," Percy's words were filled with genuine admiration.

"Thank you, Percy. I was terribly nervous, but I did my best."

It seems like you've integrated yourself back into the theatre seamlessly!" Percy placed his arm around Nancy's waist, leading her back to the dressing room, followed closely by an excited Leo.

Throughout the night, Nancy wondered where her father, Dolly, and Bill were during the opening show. She had expected them to be present, but there was no sign of them. A tinge of worry crept into her mind—had something happened to them? Tragedy and drama had plagued her life in recent months.

As Nancy approached her dressing room door, she noticed it was closed, which was unusual. The stage attendant usually left it open for easier access. The performer hesitated for a moment before reaching for the handle and then opening the door to a heartwarming surprise. Standing before her were her father, Dolly, and Bill, her father holding a bouquet.

Overwhelmed with emotion, Nancy burst into tears, rushing to embrace her family. "Oh, my goodness! I thought you hadn't come—I couldn't see you anywhere. Did you see the show?"

"Yes, Nancy. We were watching from our balcony, away from the spotlight. It was wonderful. We're so proud of you, aren't we, children?" her father beamed with pride.

"Pa, stop calling me a child! I'm nineteen now," Dolly chimed in, playfully kissing Nancy on both cheeks. "Aye, Pa, and I'm sixteen—nearly an adult. I don't want to be called a child anymore," added Bill, as Arthur affectionately tousled his hair.

Surrounded by her family's love, Nancy's heart felt lighter. She turned to Percy, a grateful smile on her face. "Did you have something to do with this?"

"Of course, I did, Nancy. Not only that, but we're off to celebrate your opening night," Percy revealed, his eyes gleaming with excitement.

Nancy's heart skipped a beat at the thought of celebrating with her loved ones, without the turmoil and demands of Robert. This time was different, and she couldn't contain her joy. "Percy, you're wonderful. I don't know what I would do without you. Did you reserve a private table, so we can dine in peace without fans interrupting us for autographs?"

But then, she caught herself. There was nothing she loved more than giving autographs and handwritten messages to her fans. It was

Robert who had cruelly discouraged such interactions, jealous and impatient with those who approached them.

"I had planned to, Nancy, but then I realised you might prefer a table in the middle of the restaurant, where your fans can see you. Would that be better?"

Nancy couldn't help but marvel at how different it was to be courted by Percy compared to Robert. She felt safe and cherished, as Percy had promised. Nancy walked up to him and wrapped her arms around his neck, a mixture of gratitude and affection in her embrace.

"You're wonderful, Percy. I can't help but wonder why you didn't enter my life sooner," her voice filled with genuine warmth.

"It just wasn't meant to be, Nancy. But what matters is that we're together now. So, as soon as you change out of your costume, shall we go and celebrate?" Percy's eyes were full of hope and anticipation.

As Nancy left the stage door, she and her loved ones were greeted by eager fans, requesting autographs and posing for photographs. Aware of the limited time and the enthusiastic crowd, Percy had arranged for two shiny black carriages to transport them to the Adelphi Theatre restaurant, a mere eight hundred yards away.

When Percy settled into the carriage beside Nancy, he exchanged a knowing glance with Leo, a hint of mischief in their eyes. Nancy questioned their secret plotting, demanding answers.

"Nothing, Nancy. And even if we were up to something, we wouldn't spoil the surprise by telling you, would we?" A mischievous grin spread across Leo's face.

The carriages arrived at the restaurant, and as they entered, the other diners gasped and turned their heads to catch a glimpse of Nancy's radiant presence. One gentleman even rose from his seat, applauding slowly, setting off a chain reaction among the other patrons. The applause subsided just as quickly, allowing Nancy and her companions to savour their meal in peace.

The waiter approached with three bottles of exquisite champagne, chilling in ice buckets. Six sparkling crystal champagne flutes accompanied the bottles, as Percy proposed a toast. He raised his glass, his eyes brimming with pride and adoration.

"Before we begin our feast, I want to express how immensely proud I am of this incredible woman. She has faced countless challenges and overcome them all. Tonight, she not only conquered her opening night but also broke records with the fastest-selling show. Nancy, I'm beyond proud of you, and I'm grateful every day that we're together."

They all raised their glasses, offering their heartfelt congratulations. "Here, here," Arthur held his glass high, reflecting the love and support that surrounded Nancy.

However, Percy had one more surprise up his sleeve. He took a step closer, reaching into his jacket's inside pocket. With anticipation and uncertainty, he retrieved a small black velvet box and placed it before Nancy. When he opened the lid, he revealed a platinum ring adorned with an oval diamond, flanked by two smaller diamonds.

Percy waited, his heart pounding, as Nancy stood up from the table, the entire room holding its breath.

Chapter Twenty-One

"I—I don't know what to say." She looked at the ring glistening in the velvet box, her mind racing with thoughts and emotions.

Percy remained standing, his eyes fixed on Nancy, his heart pounding in his chest. He had put his heart on the line, and now he awaited her response, hoping beyond hope that she would accept his proposal.

Nancy took a deep breath, feeling the weight of the moment. She looked around the table, meeting the gaze of her father, her siblings, and Leo, who all wore expressions of anticipation. Her heart swelled with love for Percy, but doubts lingered in her mind.

"Please, Nancy, take your time," Percy spoke softly, his voice filled with understanding. "I don't want you to feel rushed or pressured. I just want you to know how much you mean to me."

Nancy nodded, her eyes shimmering with unshed tears. She walked over to Percy, taking his hands in hers, feeling their warmth and strength. The room fell silent, every eye fixed on the couple in anticipation.

"You've been there for me during my darkest moments, Percy," Nancy began, her voice filled with emotion. "You've shown me kindness, love, and unwavering support. I've never felt as safe and cherished as I do when I'm with you."

A smile broke across Percy's face, hope dancing in his eyes.

"But—" Nancy's voice wavered slightly, "I need to be sure that this is what I really want. I've been hurt before. I don't want to rush into something without being certain it won't happen again."

Percy's smile softened, his hand reaching up gently to brush away a tear from Nancy's cheek. "I understand, my love. Take all the time you need. I'll be here, waiting, no matter what."

Overwhelmed with thoughts and emotions, Nancy took a step back. She looked around the table once more, seeking guidance from her loved ones. Their eyes met hers, filled with love, support, and hope.

Her gaze returned to Percy, their eyes locking, their connection unbreakable. A surge of clarity hit Nancy. The doubts began to fade, replaced by a newfound certainty.

"Yes, Percy, I would love to spend the rest of my life with you."

The room gasped with joy as Percy's face lit up. He took the ring from the box and slipped it onto Nancy's finger, sealing their love and commitment.

The room erupted into applause, the other diners joining in the celebration. Glasses were raised in a toast, and cheers filled the air. Arthur watched his daughter and fiancé, hoping for a happy ending.

Chapter Twenty-Two

The date for the wedding had been chosen, after Nancy's career had taken off and her finances had steadied. On April 20th, they would solemnly pledge their love to one another. Percy desired a grand ceremony, but Nancy hesitated. She feared being seen as just another woman who couldn't find true happiness if this marriage were to falter. He whispered promises of forever in her ear, soothing her nerves, yet Nancy's mind remained clouded with unease.

The wedding day approached, and an overwhelming anguish washed over Nancy. She yearned for her mother Jenny to be present, joining in the preparations and planning. But fate had intervened.

Death had snatched away the one woman she craved to have been closer to when she was alive.

It was up to Leo to take on the daunting task of assisting Nancy in arranging everything, from the ceremony to the breakfast. Unbeknownst to Nancy, he had secretly collaborated with Percy to plan an extravagant honeymoon once they were pronounced man and wife.

Under the radiant sun, parks bloomed with daffodils. While others went about their day, Nancy stood in her bedroom alongside Leo, who helped her dress for the occasion. He delicately placed a diamond tiara upon her head and draped a delicate lace veil across her face. Percy had gifted her pearl earrings and a shimmering diamond necklace for their special day, both of which Leo fastened with care.

Overwhelmed with joy, Nancy felt a happiness unlike anything she had experienced before. It differed vastly from her marriage to Robert, which had been born out of necessity rather than love. Nancy had been pregnant with their child and couldn't bear the scandal of having an illegitimate baby while being a public figure. She had married Robert for all the wrong reasons.

Marrying Percy, on the other hand, was a testament to pure love. However, over the past few weeks, her suspicions had grown. His songs for famous artists and Nancy's own commissions barely covered the extravagant gifts he showered upon her, and their bank account seemed to dwindle without explanation. Despite her doubts, Percy offered nothing but tenderness and unwavering love, making it impossible for her to maintain her suspicions. She wanted to believe that his actions were innocent, but the nagging fear in her mind refused to relent. She intended to address it with him after they were married, though she didn't know if it was a concern worth raising or simply an unfounded worry.

With trembling fingers, Nancy reached for the necklace while Dolly held out the lovingly crafted bouquets. The precious stones caught the light, casting myriad rainbows that danced across the walls and ceiling of Nancy's bedroom. She turned to face her sister, who wore a functional gown that hinted at her practical nature.

"I'll wear this again," Dolly grinned.

Nancy absentmindedly nodded, her focus fixed on her own reflection in the full-length mirror. She spun around, watching the ten-foot train of raw silk swish around her legs like the ebb and flow of ocean waves. Her shoes, pure white and low-heeled, peeked out from beneath the hemline.

Percy remained an enigma, but as Leo arrived in a mulberry-coloured frock coat, a white double-breasted waistcoat, and grey striped trousers, Nancy knew what to expect. The best man looked dashing.

Nancy approached her best friend, Leo, and placed a single white rose in his lapel. She then handed him his sleek, black top hat to tuck under his arm.

"Ready?" he asked with a beaming smile.

She nodded, her heart racing with excitement.

Children were absent from the wedding, and it tugged at Nancy's heart—a reminder of what might have been. There should have been a flower girl, passing her stepfather the golden ring that symbolised their love as they exchanged vows in St. Mary's. It fell upon Dolly's shoulders to safeguard the ring until they arrived.

Nancy handed her plain gold band, engraved with her initials and today's date, to her sister. "Keep this safe for us, Dolly." Nancy took a deep breath and descended the stairs, arm-in-arm with her sister, towards their waiting father. He beamed up at them from the foot of the steps.

"My beautiful daughter, you look radiant today! Percy is the perfect match for you. Any man who seeks his bride's father's permission is a true gentleman in my eyes. He will bring you endless happiness—he already has!"

Nancy stood at the threshold of her home, her heart brimming with anticipation. She smiled at her pa, sensing her mother's presence despite her absence, and tears welled up in her eyes.

Arthur sidled up beside her, his hands trembling slightly as he reached out for hers. "She'll be watching over us today, Nancy," he said. "She may not have shown it, but she loved you dearly." He opened his palm, revealing a shiny sixpence. "This is for you—it's what I neglected to give you on the day you married Robert. Perhaps that's why it ended tragically," he said, followed by a chuckle as he handed it to her.

Nancy slipped off her shoe and nestled the sixpence inside, comprehending its significance. "It's the one your mother had at our wedding, Nancy! So when you're done with it, please keep it for when your sister gets married." She gazed up at Arthur with elation. "I can't believe it—it completes the rhyme! *Something old, something new, something borrowed, something blue, and a sixpence in your shoe.* Now I know this marriage will last forever."

Leo's booming voice echoed throughout the house as he called out to Nancy, "It's time. Are you ready?" The clip-clop of two black carriages, drawn by grey horses, resonated outside the window, urging Nancy to bid farewell to the warmth and sanctuary of her home.

Stepping outside, Nancy was greeted by a chorus of cheers and applause from fans, and she beamed with delight as she waved at them. She even allowed extra time for the carriages to traverse through the throng of people, proud of this momentous occasion.

Upon arriving at their destination, Dolly gracefully led the way, guiding Nancy and Arthur towards the lychgate, where photographers and journalists eagerly awaited. Anxiety and worry had vanished, leaving only two sisters focused on helping one another celebrate this momentous day and create lasting memories.

Nancy posed for pictures with the press, eagerly expecting her photograph to grace the front pages the next morning. The sound of bells filled the air as she entered the church, arm-in-arm with her father. The pews overflowed with guests, and flowers adorned every nook and cranny of the nave. Her wedding to Percy stood in stark contrast to her marriage to Robert Wheeler. Arthur walked her down the aisle, which was lined with rose petals, as Nancy had specially requested. Percy thanked Arthur for entrusting him with his beloved daughter's hand in marriage. With teary eyes, Arthur nodded and took a seat in the front row alongside his other children. He gazed at Nancy, telling her how resplendent she looked and expressing his unwavering confidence that they would lead a splendid life together.

The vicar cleared his throat, and the entire church seemed to hold its breath. The rustling of dresses and shuffling of feet filled the air as Nancy and Percy stood side by side, ready to embark on their new life together.

Percy gazed at his bride with love in his eyes, his mouth crinkling into a smile as he beheld her beauty in the white lace gown. He reached for her hand, intertwining his fingers with hers—a silent promise that he would always be there for her.

Soft hymns filled the air as the couple exchanged vows, their hands clasped. Nancy smiled up at her husband through tear-filled eyes. Then together, they walked arm-in-arm down the aisle, grains of rice showering upon them from their benevolent well-wishers.

Dolly lifted the back of Nancy's dress as they stepped outside into the sunshine. Percy gallantly helped his new bride into the black coach drawn by four grey horses. Nancy peered out of the window, her gaze fixed on Hyde Park and their future home, while Percy held her hand.

"I have something to tell you," he began. Nancy's heart skipped a beat as she awaited his words, a twinge of apprehension coursing through her.

Chapter Twenty-Three

"This is brilliant news, my love. It's nothing but good."

Relief flooded Nancy's heart.

"I was thinking we could take a honeymoon, how about a romantic getaway?" Percy suggested.

Nancy's eyes widened, and her lips parted in disbelief. "Oh, Percy! For a moment, I thought something dreadful had happened. You've never let me down—how could I doubt you? Where are we going? And how can I possibly pack in time?"

"So many questions, Nancy! Don't fret. Your sister has handled all the packing for our trip to Venice."

Nancy gasped, wonder filling her eyes. "Venice, Percy? That would be incredible! I've never left the country before, and this is like a dream come true! How did you manage to keep it a secret for so long?"

"It was all about being careful, Nancy—with only Leo and Dolly in on it."

"Goodness, even Leo knew? He's never been one to keep surprises under wraps. You truly have been planning behind my back, Percy. I don't know what I'd do without you." Nancy looked at him, admiration in her eyes and a faint smile on her lips. She took his hand in hers, gently rubbing it as she spoke. "Percy, I'm so grateful for everything you do, not just for me, but for everyone around you. I was only teasing about not going behind my back. Now, when do we leave?"

He smiled at her tenderness, glancing at the clock before answering. "We depart right after the wedding breakfast. Dolly has prepared the outfits for our travels as well." Nancy's excitement flushed her cheeks as she realised she didn't need to worry about what to wear.

"What else do you have in store for us, Percy? Any other surprises?"

"Yes! When we return from Venice, I'm taking you to see a show at the Cambridge Theatre. I know it's something you've always wanted, so I've secured the two best seats to watch 'Haste To The Wedding.'"

Nancy gasped, clasping her hands together, tears of joy welling in her eyes. Delight coursed through her body as she tried to comprehend the boundless generosity and kindness bestowed upon her.

"What's the matter, Nancy? Why the sudden tears?"

She shook her head, wiping away a lone tear, and looked into his eyes with gratitude and love.

Nancy's heart soared as Percy spoke, and she nestled closer to him. His strong arms wrapped around her waist, offering safety and security. The warmth of his breath tickled her neck as he tenderly kissed her.

The couple sat in quiet bliss, gazing out of the carriage windows as they journeyed towards the wedding breakfast. Though they wished the moment could last forever, thoughts of their impending honeymoon drifted into their minds.

But as Nancy and Percy looked forward to the wedding breakfast, little did they know that an unforeseen twist of fate would soon cast a shadow over their romantic getaway.

Chapter Twenty-Four

"Oh, Percy! This place is wonderful!" Nancy clutched her husband's arm tightly. In the Cambridge Theatre, she was in awe of the ornate ceiling and luxurious surroundings..

They had recently returned from an unforgettable trip to Venice where they had the time of their lives. Nancy had realised during their honeymoon that she never wanted to be apart from him; he made her feel safe and loved, and that feeling was something she cherished.

Nancy was dressed in a stunning, full-length scarlet silk gown adorned with black lace around the collar. The golden chain around her neck, bedecked with pearls, sparkled for all to see. She fondly remembered picking out the pearls from a jeweller's shop in Venice as a keepsake of their time together. She had chosen them almost instantly, smiling like a child on Christmas Day.

"They're the ones!" she smiled.

The shop assistant had pointed out that matching earrings and a bracelet were available, which he advised would complete the set beautifully. Percy didn't hesitate to purchase all three. They were placed in velvet boxes and finished with stylish wrapping paper and a coloured ribbon. The gifts looked so beautiful in themselves that Nancy didn't want to open them straight away and destroy the exquisite presentation.

The large chandeliers hanging from the ornate gold-embellished ceiling above caught Nancy's eye. The lights sparkled, illuminating the vast hall that could seat fifteen hundred people. She imagined herself performing on that grand stage, basking in the limelight and receiving thunderous applause from an ecstatic audience.

"I would love to perform here one day. Do you think I will?" Nancy wondered aloud.

"I believe you can do anything you set your mind to, my love," Percy's eyes were filled with admiration.

Nancy envisioned her family and Percy sitting in the front row, witnessing her dreams come true. Nancy thought about curtsying on stage, deafened by the applause, and doing encores for an ecstatic receptive crowd who had purchased tickets well in advance. Her dream was to become a star. After sold-out shows at the Adelphi Theatre, it was time to aim higher.

"I can imagine it, Percy, and you and my family would be sitting in the front row seats."

Percy pulled out a plush velvet chair, elegantly adorned with gold leaf, and helped Nancy to her seat. The front row seats were reserved for those who paid the highest ticket prices, providing a close-up view of the performance.

"Who owns this place, Percy? Do you think we could buy it and make it our own?" Nancy's mind was busy with ambitious ideas.

Percy looked at her with a smile, amused by her boundless enthusiasm. "Well, it's not a bad idea, my dear. With your talent and my support, anything is possible." He lit a cigarette and ordered a bottle of the finest champagne. He slipped the server a tip.

"I will bring it over, Sir."

Nancy spotted the exchange of money and she gave him a nervous smile, then looked away towards the stage. Nancy had yet to solve the disappearing money from their account and would need to talk to him about it. But she was so worried that it would sound like a tyrannical diva hen-pecking her poor husband that she decided to leave it for a few more weeks. Until she had concrete proof, not suspicions.

"Look, Percy. Look! They have a revolving stage! 'Ere, I hope they don't fall off halfway through the performance and fly into the crowd," Nancy laughed at her own humour.

Percy smiled at her curiosity and knew he had married the right woman. With her beauty, kindness, care, and wealth, they would be secure for life. He delighted in watching her face soak in the experience. He would continue to watch his wife until his courage was tested when he would put his own life at risk for the sake of strangers.

After the interval, the orchestra filled the theatre with lively music, and the curtains drew back to begin the second half of the performance. Nancy's smile never wavered as she immersed herself in the show.

"Are you enjoying it, my love?" Percy was curious about her thoughts.

"Oh, Percy, I am. I can't help but think though that the songs could be better. You could write much more captivating tunes than these. Why don't you talk to them about it?"

Percy chuckled at Nancy's suggestion, and even the table next to them seemed to agree. "Well, perhaps I will," he said playfully.

As they sat back and enjoyed the show, little did they know that the night at the Cambridge Theatre held more surprises for them. A dramatic chain of events would capture the city's attention by the evening's end.

Chapter Twenty-Five

As the second half of the performance was about to start on the grand stage, Nancy's heart swelled with artistic dreams, her eyes sparkling with curiosity. She couldn't help but wonder who owned this enchanting theatre, the mastermind behind the captivating acts that graced the hallowed boards.

Leaning towards her husband, Percy, she whispered, "Percy, who's the genius behind this place? I bet they've got an eye for talent like ours. It would be a dream to know who selects the acts that grace this magical stage."

Percy grinned, sharing her excitement, and replied, "Well, I heard they've been trying to sell it to the London Metropolitan Borough, but the ratepayers keep putting a stop to it. Who knows what'll happen next? I just hope this beautiful theatre doesn't end up lost to time."

Nancy's curiosity burned brighter than ever, fuelling her dreams of one day stealing the spotlight on that very stage. "That's a shame. It's such a beautiful place. I'd hate to see it demolished or just sit here and become dilapidated. Who would be without a theatre such as this?" Nancy sighed, her eyes wandering around the elegant venue.

The waitress brought another bottle of champagne just as the orchestra started playing again. Nancy couldn't believe how happy she was, and she didn't want the enchanting evening to end.

The brass section played loudly, drowning out any muffled sounds and the clinking of champagne glasses as the performers got ready for the next scenes. The audience settled down, and it felt like the whole theatre was quiet, waiting in anticipation of the rest of the show.

Percy noticed something moving in the corner of his eye. He looked up and noticed a drunken spectator standing up and starting to shout at the woman sitting opposite him. His heart started beating faster, and he clenched his fists, trying not to let his anger get the better of him. But it was no use. He had seen this thing once too often. Memories of Mr Wilson standing over his mother, threatening her with his fist, came flooding back.

Percy stood up and walked over to the corner table where the argument was taking place, crouching down as low as possible so as not to disturb anybody else. Nancy watched her husband stand up and move away from where they were sitting. She, too, caught the movement of the man pointing his finger down at the woman in front of him.

The star didn't need the orchestra to be quiet to notice the way he was talking to her.

"Excuse me, sir, why don't you leave this woman alone and just sit down and enjoy the performance?" Percy said, trying to intervene calmly.

"How dare you tell me how to behave!" the stranger retorted, his voice slurred.

By this point, the orchestra had quietened to a 'calando', so all attention was on Percy and the stranger. The woman looked more uncomfortable by the minute, leaning as far back in her chair as possible, as if trying to move further away from the hurtful words and the threat of violence.

"There really is no need for that attitude, sir. All I'm asking is that you sit down and enjoy the rest of the show like everybody else. And perhaps consider treating your lady friend here with a bit more respect," Percy urged, his voice firm.

"What did you say—"

Suddenly, the stranger pulled back his fist and thrust it forward towards Percy's right cheekbone. Nancy gasped in horror, but her husband managed to duck, avoiding the stranger's knuckles. The gentleman wobbled unsteadily on his feet, his cigarette flying through the air as he fell back towards the table. The tall, slim woman, dressed in her stunning emerald-green dress, stood up and moved out of the way just before the table fell on her.

Percy stepped backward as the two candlesticks fell and caught the edge of the white tablecloth. A black rim smouldered slowly, burning the hem away. Spreading quickly, it set the tablecloth alight. Soon, it had jumped across some velvet door coverings.

Nancy looked up towards a hysterical woman wailing over at the other side of the auditorium, in the first row of the balcony. She opened her mouth, and a high-pitched scream filled the theatre, followed by the terrifying words:

"Fire! Quick! Fire!"

Chapter Twenty-Six

Percy noticed people running to the back of the theatre, screaming and shouting. Entertainers ran off stage and left through the nearest exit. The conductor and musicians grabbed what they could before fleeing with their valuable instruments through another back entrance.

"This is tragic!" Percy clasped either side of his face with his hands, his mouth wide open at the horror in front of him.

"Percy! Percy! Quick, hurry! We need to get out!" screamed Nancy.

Hartman ran over to his wife and begged her to leave. "I need to help these people. This is my fault! You go, Nancy, and I will follow you. Quickly, leave."

"I'm not leaving without you, Percy". " I'll be fine, Nancy, just go." He ran into the immediate crowd urging them to leave. The flames now licked hungrily around more of the dining furniture.

He helped the women first run towards the front of the theatre, their husbands, fiancés, brothers, and fathers all following in a mad panic. Percy shouted at the spectators to run for their lives as he watched the theatre burn around him.

"Come, Nancy, this way!" She didn't know who had grabbed her by her arms. She looked back and shouted for her husband, who was desperately trying to save people. "Perrcccyyyyy!"

But her desperate cries for her husband were not heard by him. It's like she was lifted off her feet by the sea of people as they flooded onto the streets. Some were desperately trying to gasp for air. Nancy was outside looking at the theatre and bit her nails until the nail wicks started to bleed.

I need to go back in! She made a run for it, fighting through the crowds which were travelling in the opposite direction until a gentleman grabbed her.

"No, you don't, Miss. It's far too dangerous."

"But my husband! He's in there helping others escape."

"That's why you should stay out here. There are too many people in there already, they are hampering our rescue efforts."

Nancy knew he was right. There was nothing for her to do but wait for Percy to emerge from the theatre, either on foot or on a stretcher. She looked up to the sky and noticed smoke billowing out of the roof. The streets and pavements were filled with theatregoers who had toppled out onto the cobbles. Some had black faces from the smoke. Women and men searched for loved ones in the crowd.

"Please, God, please, let Percy and everyone else be safe," she whispered to herself. It seemed like the whole London Fire Brigade had arrived, hastily unravelling the hundreds of yards of hose carried on each carriage. Firefighters dressed in double-breasted serge tunics and brass helmets were tightening fixings on the hoses with their spanners. They entered the theatre with axes for breaking doors.

The shouts and screams from the crowds were so loud she could barely think. Losing Percy now filled her with dread. "Please, God, it's too soon to lose him. I've only just found my happiness," she croaked.

She stood on her tiptoes, trying to see across a deep sea of heads and shoulders. Everybody was tightly squashed together, so finding anybody was made so much more difficult. Musicians held their instruments close to them as if they were their life. People cried on the shoulders of others. The performers, still in their costumes, hugged one another and wrapped their arms around each other's necks and shoulders for comfort.

The fire turned the sky orange as it took hold on the roof. Percy was nowhere to be seen. "Excuse me, my husband is in there helping others escape. Please can you go find him?"

The fireman just shook his head. "Sorry, Miss. Please get out of the way so we can do our job. We will do our best to rescue him." He ran with his hose towards the theatre as Nancy stood frozen to the spot, losing all hope she would ever see Percy alive again. Her emotions got the better of her, and she fell to her knees on the cold, hard cobbles, crying her beloved's name out over and over again.

The crowd started to disperse. Loved ones stumbled away from the worst night of their lives, supporting each other. Nancy watched women cry into their handkerchiefs and wailing to their loved ones they would never recover from this dreadful night.

The survivors leaving the theatre dwindled, and Percy was nowhere to be found. Occasionally, a sheet-covered body on a stretcher would pass by her. 'Dear God, bless their souls.' Nancy watched the firefighters run in and out of the building and prayed every time they carried someone out alive that it was Percy.

Those members of the public lucky enough to run out of the burning theatre unaided stopped, leaned on their knees with their hands and tried to catch a breath. Terrified, she hoped to never witness such a sight again. The lonely star stared at the doors. She tenderly stroked the bracelet Percy had brought her in Italy and clung on to it tightly for hope.

As she watched the building for movement, she remembered her honeymoon in Venice. It had been the best month of her life. They had sat in fine restaurants drinking expensive wine and eating food they had never heard of before. The newlyweds walked the canals holding hands and stealing unnoticed kisses.

She remembered their last evening in the European city with gladness in her heart. The words were etched into her memory. "I love you, Mrs Hartman. May we have magical years to come."

"I love you too, Percy. I still can't believe you are mine." They spoke late into the night about future shows and how one day, Percy hoped he could take care of her financially.

"Oh, Percy! You have done enough for me already. It doesn't matter that I earn most of the money. I'm happy to share it. As long as we are together, that's all that matters."

Amidst the wet cobbles and shouting firemen, Nancy brought herself back to the present moment. She was devastated to see her new family and future burning away before her eyes.

"Don't worry, little one. We will be okay." She rubbed her belly tenderly where their child lay, unaware of the goings-on outside. Nancy hadn't had a chance to tell Percy that he was going to be a father.

"Why me?" She said, as she looked down at her belly. "Why us? Why can't we just be normal?"

"Excuse me! Move, casualty coming through!"

Nancy noticed two firemen bringing out a body on a stretcher. Her heart started beating faster as she ran across the cobbles, nearly twisting her ankle in haste. She saw the man lying unconscious before her. "Percy!"

Chapter Twenty-Seven

Golden sunlight pierced through the slender opening between the deep emerald velvet curtains, rousing Nancy from a shallow yet weighty slumber that had seized her in the twilight hours. After the restful darkness, her eyes took their time adjusting to the daylight.

Nancy had navigated her way to her deserted and lonely home in the small hours of the morning. With her mind on Percy and whether he would survive, she was unaware of the damage done to her. The once splendid gown, torn and smeared with soot, hung on her body while her chestnut curls, dishevelled and greasy, tumbled across her face. She had battled her way out of the catastrophe, her skin grubby and rough, leaving her exhausted and deflated about what the future held for her.

Yet, she had dragged herself upstairs to their bedroom, tumbling onto the bed. Her shoes were the only things she had the energy to remove. Her attire and jewellery clung to her worn and battered form as she sank into the bed, drawing the covers up to her chin.

As her body stirred, signs of the previous night's horror surfaced. An acrid taste stung the back of her throat, her eyes smarted, and a soft choking sound slipped from her lips. The scenes from the calamity came back to her in fleeting, sharp flashes as she tried to shake them away, only to have tears streak through the soot on her face, marking clean paths down her cheeks.

"Percy," she whispered into the silent room. "How would I cope without you? Without you by my side, my life would never be the same."

In brighter times, the morning sun would have urged them out of bed for a jaunt in the park or a leisurely breakfast at one of London's finest patisseries. Today, however, the sunlight only deepened her sorrow, the gaping void left by her absent husband stark and tangible.

A crushing sensation of impending doom wrapped itself around her as she grappled with the injustice of her fate. Shoving the cotton bedsheets and embroidered quilt away, she planted her feet on the plush rug at the bedside. Standing up, she noticed the ash tarnished the white cotton bedsheet and smoke ingrained in her clothing.

Moving with measured steps towards the window, she attempted to untangle her hair before her fingers stroked the string of pearls still adorning her neck.

Although Nancy was aware she had to remain hopeful for Percy to pull through, the uncertainty of his condition weighed on her. At the hospital, the doctor had denied her entry, saying that immediate surgery was required. Concealed by a sheet, Percy's arrival was marked by the horrifying sight of blood seeping through. Despite her pleas, they would not let her stay with him.

"Mrs Hartman, we must attend to your husband," the doctor had insisted. "Please, do both yourself and your husband a favour and rest. Should he pull through, he will need you strong for his recovery."

The journey from St Thomas' to their home usually called for a carriage, but that night, she desired the night air's chill. Walking home, she could process the magnitude of what had happened.

The mystery of her dwindling bank balance, noticeable since her return from the Italian tour, occupied her thoughts. She had meant to discuss it with Percy after the show, but fate had intervened.

She shook herself back to the present, her stomach growling. She touched her belly, the reminder of her pregnancy filling her with mixed emotions. *How could I have forgotten I am carrying our child?* She soothed herself, acknowledging the trauma she had just survived. She had always longed for a family with Percy, but now their child's father fought for his life.

Nancy undressed, cleaned herself, and slipped into simpler attire suited for the tasks ahead. As she rinsed the washcloth in warm water, she noticed the lines of soot etched into her face. Pulling at her skin, she stared at herself in the mirror, pondering the string of calamities she had weathered. She dreamed of a day filled with the laughter of children and Percy's playful pursuits. However, the cruel reality was that she did not know whether Percy was alive.

As the tears started to fall again, she steeled herself. "Stay strong, Nancy. For you, and for Percy," she wiped her tears away with the warm washcloth. She dried herself off, tossed the towel on the bed, and pulled on a sensible brown tweed skirt, a white blouse, and a green cardigan from her wardrobe. She slipped into comfortable shoes that would carry her a distance without hurting her feet.

Her stomach grumbled again, signalling the urgency of a meal. Noticing the lack of cash in her purse, she went to the drawing room and opened the drawer of the mahogany desk where they kept the money tin.

Holding the tin next to her ear and hearing no jingle of coins, she hoped to find notes instead. *If there are notes in here, it would mean he hasn't left me penniless.* However, she felt her hopes shatter when she opened the tin and found it empty.

"What are you doing with our money, Percy?" she wondered aloud. She threw the tin back into the drawer, slamming it shut, and stormed out of the room. She grabbed her carpet bag, signalling the start of a new chapter in her life. But still, the question remained. What would become of Percy, and where had their money gone?

Chapter Twenty-Eight

⁓⁓⁕⁓⁓

Nancy was acutely aware that she'd have to stroll by the remnants of the Cambridge Theatre to reach the bank. She needed money to buy some food for herself and her soon-to-be-born child and had no money to pay her staff to do it for her.

"Come and get your paper!" The boy who always sold newspapers stood at the bustling intersection of Hyde Park and The Aldwych. "Latest paper, Miss! All about the tragedy, those lost and those who made it!"

Nancy was troubled by the boy's indifferent tone about an incident that would scar so many. His face wore a grin as he noticed her gaze.

"Sure you don't need one, Miss?"

She almost snapped at him. He had no idea that she'd spent several hours watching the theatre burn. Nor did he know that one of the victims, her husband, had been dragged from the ruins, barely alive.

"I'll get one later, thank you," she replied, her gaze barely meeting his. The thought of an empty purse felt like a heavy stone in her pocket.

As she neared the theatre, the pungent scent of charred wood filled her nostrils. The stench hadn't entirely faded since she'd left the dreadful scene in the early hours. She felt the temperature rising as she drew closer to the remains of the theatre, but the horrific images of the previous night sent a cold shiver down her spine, replacing the warmth with dread.

Despite not wanting to look at the ruin, she found herself stopping and staring. The clean-up operation was still underway. The smoke twisted upwards from the smouldering debris of the theatre. Now it was just the firemen present who were busy dampening down the last remnants of the flames. It led her to assume that either all the victims had been found or there was no hope of finding any more survivors.

The theatre had been reduced to a mound of rubble with charred timber protruding from heated bricks and stone. Firefighters navigated the debris, moving searing wood and bricks aside. Occasional shouts echoed from the wreckage followed by a moment of silence to listen for any signs of life beneath.

Every so often, she'd notice a firefighter closing his eyes, shaking his head at the devastation. The disaster would leave an indelible mark on the city's memory. Nancy spotted a woman frantically searching for something on the ground and approached her. "Pardon me, miss. Are you alright? Can I help you?"

The woman looked up at Nancy, startled. Her eyes were bloodshot and she was covered in soot. Her hair looked neglected, and her clothes were torn. She paused her search to respond.

"I've lost my earrings. Can't find them anywhere!" She looked back down, resuming her hunt through the charred rubble.

Nancy knelt down and started to help. "Were you here alone, or did you come with someone?"

"My husband brought me. He's at home now. He seems more upset about my lost earrings than the lives lost. I didn't agree with him about coming back here, but I'd rather look for the earrings than face his wrath."

Nancy was immediately reminded of her past experiences with Robert, the bruises she had to hide, and the hurt she had endured. "I'm sorry," she said, rising to her feet, "I can't help you further. I need to see my husband in the hospital. And perhaps, if your husband cares more about earrings than people's lives, you should find a new one."

The woman stopped searching, looking up in shock at Nancy's words.

Nancy wasn't one for frankness, but with last night's events and an uncertain future, she had little patience for those concerned more with material things than human lives.

She finished her walk to the bank, reflecting on her life with Percy. Had she noticed any signs that would justify him withdrawing from their joint account without asking her? But nothing came to mind, except the honeymoon.

Percy had no involvement in their wedding's expenditure, so the only lavish expenditure she could think of was their trip to Italy. Nancy struggled to decide how to bring up this issue with Percy, who seemed to be on his deathbed. She didn't want to accuse him as she had Robert, but she couldn't help suspecting Percy of foul play.

How am I supposed to discuss this with him when he's barely hanging on? For all I know, he might not even have made it through the night, making this entire ordeal pointless. Nancy continued to the bank in a daze. She recognised one of the clerks who always treated her with kindness.

"Miss Franklin, how are you today? You've heard about the terrible fire, haven't you?"

Nancy didn't really want to talk about it, but she felt cornered. "Yes, I was there. It was horrific. I passed the building just now, it's just a pile of smouldering rubble. I can't imagine it ever being rebuilt, nor can I bear the thought of the lives lost."

"Oh, Miss Franklin, that's terribly sad. Please sit down, I'll get you a cup of tea." Instead of leading her to the counter, the clerk, Miss Dawson, led Nancy to a more private desk behind a partition. "So, Miss Franklin, what can I help you with today?"

"It's a bit complicated. I just need to check the balance of our joint account. I've noticed some substantial expenditures over the past months. I'm sure it's nothing serious. Percy loves to surprise me now and then. But I need to withdraw some money for groceries while Percy is in the hospital."

Miss Dawson was taken aback. "Oh dear, is Percy in the hospital due to the fire?"

Nancy nodded, dabbing her eyes with a tissue from her bag.

"I'm very sorry to hear that. Let's get this done quickly so you can visit him." Miss Dawson retrieved their account ledger and began to review the transactions.

It didn't take long for Nancy to notice the concern etched on the clerk's face. "Whatever it is, Miss Dawson, you can tell me. I'm almost prepared for the account to be empty."

"Well, Miss Franklin," the young woman started, removing her glasses, "I'm relieved to say there is money in the account, but it is very little considering how much you have deposited."

Nancy sighed and braced herself for what Miss Dawson was about to say.

"It was almost at zero when your previous husband died, and I know you have worked hard to build it back up since then." She left a couple of seconds' silence before continuing. "But I'm afraid to say over the past six months, there have been certain sizeable transactions, shall we say, that I'm not sure you are aware of. Otherwise, I don't think you would be sitting here in front of me today asking these questions."

Nancy mentally prepared herself for the worst news financially. Not only did the outcome not look good for her new husband, who she was so madly in love with, but it looked like there was little in the account. She started to feel physically sick at the thought of her money dwindling yet again, swindled by somebody she thought loved her.

She had trusted Percy implicitly enough to marry the man after a few short months. But now, she just felt he had been dishonest and cruel in the most hurtful way. "Why don't you just tell me what the current position is, and where the money has gone, and we can take it from there."

The woman opposite popped her glasses back on and started to read out their withdrawal transactions. "In total, there have been fifteen transactions in the past six months, Miss Franklin, leaving you with a balance in the account of just—" She hesitated again before finishing the sentence. "Five hundred pounds."

Nancy felt her heart sink. Her shoulders noticeably drooped in front of the clerk before her.

"In fact, it appears that every time the account breached that balance, the money was withdrawn immediately, leaving exactly five hundred pounds in the account each time."

"Thank you, Miss Dawson. Please could I withdraw five pounds just now."

The clerk knew not to press Nancy any further into how she was going to tackle this new information. Instead, she handed over the money and gave the actress a sympathetic smile.

The devastated performer stood up and left the bank. When she got out, she wondered how quickly her life had turned into a heart-breaking mess again. Her husband had lied to her, and who knew where the money was.

Chapter Twenty-Nine

Nancy was unsure how to ask him about the missing money. But with a child on the way, which Percy didn't yet know about, she was going to have to get to the bottom of the disappearing cash.

I've been strong before and survived, and I can do it again, she muttered as she made her way to St Thomas'.

She had more important matters to attend to before visiting her father and siblings to inform them of what had happened.

Nancy stared at the piece of paper with her measly account balance written on in pencil. How would she handle the shocking truth of her dying husband's theft?

Nancy made her way back through the city, the oppressive heat of the afternoon sun left her feeling light-headed. The streets were filled with noise and chaos, but her own thoughts drowned it all out. She felt a peculiar sense of solitude, despite being in the heart of the bustling city.

Arriving at the hospital, she steeled herself for the sight that might meet her. She stopped at the entrance, drawing a deep breath and bolstering her nerves before pushing through the large double doors. As she walked down the dimly lit corridors, the distinctive smell of antiseptic hit her nostrils, creating a knot of unease in her stomach.

Nancy made her way to Percy's bedside, where he lay unconscious, bandages swathed around his face and arms. The sight of him stirred a storm of emotions within her: worry, resentment, love, and anger all swirling together into a tumultuous mess. He looked fragile, defenceless; a stark contrast to the strong, vibrant man she had married.

"Percy?" she whispered, a trembling hand reaching out to touch his. "It's Nancy."

There was no response, no squeeze of his hand or flutter of his eyelids. Just the steady rhythm of his chest rising and falling again.

Nancy sat down on the chair next to Percy's bed, taking his limp hand in hers. She desperately wanted to tell him about their baby, about the dwindling bank account, about her fears and doubts. But she couldn't. Not yet. With nothing else to do, she held his hand and hoped.

The hours passed, accompanied by the steady tick of the wall clock and the soft rustle of the nurses in the background. Each passing moment felt like an eternity, the wait agonisingly slow.

The thoughts of their dwindling bank account loomed heavy in her mind. The questions, the doubts, the worry were like a dull ache that refused to leave her. But she pushed them aside, focusing on the man lying in front of her.

Suddenly, there was a subtle change in Percy. A soft groan escaped his lips, his eyebrows furrowed, and his hand tightened around Nancy's. His eyelids fluttered open, revealing cloudy, pain-filled eyes.

"Percy?" Nancy leaned in, searching his face for any sign of recognition.

His gaze moved around the room before landing on her. His lips parted, a whisper of a word escaping him. "Nancy?"

Her heart thudded against her ribcage, relief washing over her. "Yes, Percy, it's me. You're in the hospital, but you're going to be okay."

A smile tugged at the corners of Percy's mouth, but it quickly faded, replaced by a grimace of pain. His grip on her hand tightened as he fought against the pain that wracked his body. "The theatre—" he whispered, his voice raspy and filled with confusion.

Nancy nodded, gently squeezing his hand. "Yes, there was a fire. But you made it out. You're alive."

A distant look came into Percy's eyes, his gaze unfocused. He was silent for a moment, lost in his thoughts. Then he looked at Nancy, a profound sadness filling his eyes. "I'm sorry, Nancy."

"Sorry?" she asked, her voice barely above a whisper.

Before he could answer, a wave of exhaustion washed over him, his eyes fluttering shut as he fell into a restless sleep.

Nancy was left with even more questions, her heart filled with confusion and worry. What was Percy sorry about? Was he referring to the money? Did he know about it? Or was it something else entirely?

Nancy sat in the dimly lit hospital room, the seeds of doubt and fear planted in her heart began to grow, painting a picture of uncertainty and hardship. A story was just beginning, a chapter waiting to unfold.

Looking down at Percy sleeping, she couldn't help but feel sorry for him. But, she also knew that she may be facing a future without him.

She leaned back in the chair, her gaze still on Percy. The fight was far from over. As night approached, new challenges emerged. But Nancy was determined. She had been through a lot, and she was ready to face whatever came her way.

She would wait for Percy to wake up, for answers, for her life to make sense again.

Whatever happened next, Nancy knew that she had to be ready. But for now, she would wait. In the quiet stillness of the hospital room, she held Percy's hand, her thoughts a whirlwind of fear and hope. The future was uncertain, the path ahead rocky. But as long as she had breath in her body, she would fight. For Percy, for their unborn child, and for herself.

And only time would tell what the future held for her.

Chapter Thirty

Nancy's heart was set on the one place where she could find solace and love. She took a deep breath, mustering her strength for the journey back to her childhood home. Her steps quickened, pounding on the pavement as she wrestled with her thoughts, moving from one distressing realisation to another. The fire had separated her from her family, and a gnawing panic gripped her chest. They must be worried sick about me. I need to see them.

She averted her gaze from the passersby on the street, eventually reaching the weathered double gates, caked in mud and filth, at the entrance of the courtyard.

THE STARLET SLUM GIRL

Familiar faces greeted her with smiles, hungry for details about the fire and the latest scoop on her tumultuous day. She couldn't spare a moment, striding towards her father's door, brushing aside stares and attempts to interrupt.

Without knocking, she entered. Her unexpected appearance stunned her family, their surprise mirrored in their eyes when they saw the turmoil etched on her face.

"Tell us about your honeymoon—"

Nancy cut off her father's words, launching into a rapid recounting of the events, her breaths shallow and hurried.

Percy and I watched 'Haste to the Wedding' at the Cambridge Theatre last night."

Gasps escaped from the mouths of her family. The inferno had been the talk of the town and her family had no idea she had been a part of it.

"Oh, my word, Nancy, are you—"

"The second half was about to start when Percy noticed something from the corner of his eye. I saw a man arguing with his wife, and Percy stepped in. Then everything went horribly wrong. The candlesticks crashed down as the man tried to hit Percy. That's how the fire began. I begged him to leave as the flames spread, but he refused. He said there were lives to save, and I should wait outside."

Bill, usually a young man of few words, spoke up in support.

"Well, I reckon that's remarkable, Nancy. A fine thing he did. You should be proud of him."

She raised her finger to silence her brother as she continued her tale. "Next thing, I saw him being carried out on a stretcher, unsure if he was alive or dead, blood staining the sheets."

"Have you seen him?"

Nancy gazed at her father in a daze. "Yes, I have, but he's barely conscious. He can't talk."

"Oh, Nancy. That's terrible."

Sitting at the table where they once shared suppers, her heart heavy, Nancy's sister Dolly started to cry. She wondered if her sister would ever catch a break in her tumultuous life. "It's so dreadful, Nancy. Do you think he will be okay?"

"His chances of survival are uncertain, despite the doctors' optimism."

Arthur, her father, came over and embraced her, holding her as she released her pent-up tears. Shaking from the surge of emotions, Nancy pushed her father away, gathering the courage to share another piece of news.

"But there's more. This morning, I went to the bank to get money for food. The clerk said our account had shrunk considerably compared to what was deposited. Percy's been withdrawing large sums for six months without my knowledge." Nancy covered her face, weighed down by the events of the past day. Arthur slammed his fist on the wobbly table, making everyone jump and the teapot lid rattle.

"The scoundrel. How dare he treat you like that, after what Robert did? I thought he was trustworthy, but I was wrong. You have every reason to be upset." Arthur stared at the floor, rubbing his forehead, grappling with the shocking revelation. He deliberated on Nancy's next move.

"He can't take from you without asking. You've worked hard. Don't let this slip away, no matter his state."

"But what should I do? Where to start?"

"Find out if he's done this before. See if he's a fraudster, a narcissist. If he is, report him. Even if you're the first victim, report him."

Nancy's anxiety gnawed at her. She longed for simplicity.

"He's written music for others, start there. Seek out the music hall stars. Hasn't he managed acts?"

Nancy nodded, sighing at the daunting task ahead.

Arthur couldn't bear to see his daughter in so much pain. He waited for her response, biting his lip. Nancy cried again as she shared her latest news.

"But that's not all. It's not just me now." Tears flowed down Nancy's cheeks, landing on her chin and chest. A silence fell upon the room.

Arthur wasn't one to cry in front of his children, aside from Jenny's death. His gaze shifted to Nancy's pregnant belly and he cried thinking of the road ahead for his daughter, who'd seen so much sorrow. In that moment, Arthur vowed that Percy Hartman would pay for hurting his daughter, regardless of his condition, whether he lay dying in a hospital bed or not.

Chapter Thirty-One

It had been a long, emotionally draining four days since Nancy had tried to visit Percy again in the hospital. She had thought of nothing but her beloved husband lying burnt and scarred since she left St Thomas'. Her worry for Percy's survival had caused her to bite down her fingernails until they bled.

After Nancy left her father's house that night, she bought a newspaper on the way home and started searching for the stars who she remembered Percy claimed he had written music for. She hoped to find them performing in a show and scouted the advertisements and theatre posters plastered on doorways and lampposts.

All she wanted to do was talk to one of the performers to either confirm or deny whether what she was thinking about her husband was true or not. Maybe they could shed light on whether he had stolen from them, too.

The star grew tired of imagining the worst for her marriage, suspecting Percy of embezzlement. She didn't think she could stand being defrauded by another husband. Nancy yearned for clarity, to finally make a decision and move forward, with or without him.

The newspapers were still reporting on the Cambridge Theatre fire. She wondered how the journalists got hold of so much information and found enough to write about one event for five consecutive days.

"THREE DEAD IN CAMBRIDGE FIRE BUT MANY LIVES SAVED THANKS TO NANCY'S HUSBAND!"
"PERFORMERS AND FANS WATCH ON IN HORROR AS THEATRE BURNS TO THE GROUND!"
"LIVES CHANGED FOREVER AS HUNDREDS ESCAPE THEATRE FIRE!"
"THEATRE GOERS DIE AS THE CAMBRIDGE BECOMES A BLAZING INFERNO!"

She tried to avoid reading the horrific details, but one headline caught her attention.

"HERO OF THE NIGHT SAVES HUNDREDS OF LIVES AS HE RACES AGAINST TIME TO RESCUE CAMBRIDGE FIRE VICTIMS!"

Theatre goers, who were just about to enjoy the second half of the performance of 'Haste To The Wedding', fled for their lives as a blaze quickly took hold inside the Cambridge Theatre.

The fire trapped many people inside, leading to the death of three individuals. However, Percy Hartman's bravery prevented the number of casualties from being much higher.

Better known as Nancy Franklin's husband, according to eyewitness reports and the London Fire Brigade, Hartman selflessly stayed in the theatre to help trapped theatregoers escape from the blazing inferno. Firefighters tried desperately to dampen the flames, and the hero of the night could be seen being stretchered out of the burning building, covered in a blood-soaked sheet. We do not know his current condition, but it is believed that he will have life-changing burns on his body.

As she read the newspaper article, it made her think that her own private investigation into where the money had disappeared to, was turning out to be less important than she had originally told herself.

Nancy sat down at her dressing table and looked at the wood-framed mirror as she brushed her hair with the green enamelled back hairbrush. The soft white bristles gently teased the bedtime knots out, and she noticed she had started to get the gloss back on her long brown locks. No visible signs remained on her body from that devastating night. Just emotional scars that she would need to heal before returning to the stage without a fear the theatre would go up in flames.

Nancy missed her husband terribly, even though she knew there was a chance that he had betrayed her. He had shown her what it was like to feel loved and to love unconditionally. Some of the happiest days of her life had been spent with him. The thought of not seeing him again brought tears to her eyes.

She fastened the pearls around her neck, wishing that he was behind her doing it instead. He would take each end of the necklace and fasten it, finishing with a tender, light kiss on her skin. Nancy stared into space and imagined his tender touch. The bereft performer felt her hands ache with the desire to hold her husband close and feel his warmth. Nancy shivered as she felt a sudden cool breeze wrap around her. It brought her back to her senses and made her finish getting ready to go and see the show.

After spending hours searching for the names, she remembered Percy mentioning someone in particular. She ran her finger down the flyer and noticed that The Black Domino was showing tonight at the Adelphi Theatre starring Agnes Berridge. She brought her fingertips to her mouth and bit her bottom lip.

Nancy was excited about going for various reasons. It would cast her fears aside of the same thing ever happening again at a theatre, and she was hoping she could catch Agnes after the performance to make some private enquiries into Percy's musical background.

She stood up from her mahogany-polished dressing table and walked over to Percy's few vinyl records, which he kept in alphabetical order on the bottom shelf of the bookcase. Fancying some music to get her in the mood for the show, she pulled out a vinyl from its sleeve and placed it on the gramophone's round rubber plate. She cranked it up to speed and placed the needle between the grooves.

Standing by the window, she immersed herself in the music, briefly tilting her head to the side as a sign of familiarity washed over her. *Hang on a moment, I'm sure this is one of the songs in the show tonight!* She turned the record sleeve over, reading the credits on the back.

'*Sung by Agnes—Originally performed in The Black Domino.*'

I'm sure I've heard something similar before!

Nancy tapped her foot and clicked her fingers, trying to get the beat of the music, and as she did so, some words naturally came to her. *I don't believe it. It sounds almost identical to 'My Old Man Loves Me' that I've sang many a time before.*

Nauseous at the new discovery, she stomped her feet like a petulant child, wishing she hadn't played the record. *How dare he fob us both off like that!* She grabbed her bag from the hall console and walked out of her house, slamming the door behind her. *Just you wait until I see that strumpet!* Nancy was starting to panic that if her worst fears were true, her father would bring his verbal threat to life.

"I promise you, Nancy, if I find out he has ever stolen from my daughter, I will have his guts for garters and make sure he goes down forever!"

The words that had previously come out of Arthur's mouth did nothing to dampen her suspicions. She feared for Percy's safety if her father ever caught up with him, remembering her pa's venomous words. She wanted Percy to recover and for her suspicious mind to have lied to her. Nancy wanted nothing more but to raise a family and be happy until their dying days. She had believed Percy to be the one as soon as she met him, so she prayed to God that he hadn't let her down.

Her chest started tightening with anxiety as she stepped inside the grand Adelphi Theatre. She looked around and saw other theatregoers nervously looking over their shoulders. She took some deep breaths and found her seat and sat down next to a married couple who were holding hands and looking into each other's eyes.

The orchestra started to play as the theatre usher shone his torch on seat numbers, so the final stragglers could take their seats quickly, minimising any disruption to other spectators. There was, of course, no need for Nancy to feel anxious. The show passed without any drama and she could hear sighs of relief as the performance ended.

The conductor turned around to face the audience and took a bow as the orchestra stood on their feet, some holding their instruments in the air as if to celebrate the end of the first performance in a theatre since the fire.

Just before the end of the encore, Nancy apologised to her row of spectators as she tried to get past them to make her way to the stage door to wait for the cast to leave. The panic started rising in her chest as her eyes scanned the theatre for any sign of trouble. But there was nothing. Only theatre-goers enjoying themselves.

After half an hour, the crowd had got slightly bigger, but she had kept her position just to the left of the door as the cast appeared and flooded out into the alleyway at the side of the theatre. She quickly recognised Agnes, who was dressed in normal clothes and without make-up, after seeing her picture in an interview published in The Times.

Nancy almost lost sight of her as Agnes hurried through the crowd, trying to escape the fans who had waited patiently for autographs. *Mmm, she's not as keen or happy as me to oblige.*

"Agnes? Agnes! Excuse me, Agnes? The performer turned around and stared at who she thought was a persistent fan wanting a piece of her valuable time.

"Nancy? Nancy Franklin? What on earth are you doing here?"

Chapter Thirty-Two

※

In the dimly lit hospital room, Percy lay on his bed, his body still bearing the painful marks of the recent fire. As he glanced around the room, his eyes caught a glimpse of his nurse, Alice. She had a comforting aura about her, and something in her features seemed familiar. However, Percy brushed the thought away, attributing it to the lingering confusion from the accident.

Alice, on the other hand, appeared preoccupied, her mind seemingly elsewhere. In a moment of carelessness, she accidentally brushed against Percy's burns while dressing them.

"Ouch!" Percy exclaimed, wincing at the sudden pain.

"Sorry, sorry!" Alice apologised, flustered. "My mind's a bit all over the place today."

Percy grinned, trying to ease her distress. "No problem. You seem a little bothered about something. Are you okay?"

Alice hesitated but then found herself trusting the patient before her. "Well, I've received a letter from home," she began, her voice tinged with worry. "My mother is gravely ill, and I need to visit her."

"Your mother? What's her name?" Percy asked, curiosity piqued.

"Kitty," Alice replied, her gaze distant as she spoke of her mother's condition.

In that moment, Percy's heart skipped a beat, and his mind raced to the past. Could it be possible? Was this nurse his long-lost sister? The one he thought he had lost forever? Impossible. His sister's name was Grace, not Alice.

Summoning his courage, Percy took a deep breath. "Do you have any siblings, Alice?"

"Yes," Alice nodded, her eyes glistening with emotion. "I had a brother, Peter. He disappeared though after something happened to us all when I was a lot younger. No one has seen him since."

Percy felt a mixture of emotions swirling within him. He sensed a connection. And then it dawned on him, the faded memories returning to haunt him. Taking a deep breath, he gathered his courage and whispered, "Alice, I need to tell you something. My real name is Peter. Do you think we could be—No, ignore me. I'm being stupid."

"Go on, Alice said encouragingly. What were you going to say?" She could feel her heart thumping heavily in her chest as her temperature rose.

"I was going to say, do you think we could be related? My ma's name was Katherine, but my sister was called Grace, not Alice."

Alice's eyes widened with surprise, and then tears welled up in her eyes. "Peter?" she choked out, her voice trembling. "Is it really you?"

Percy nodded, his heart pounding in his chest. "Yes, it's me," he affirmed, feeling a wave of relief and apprehension wash over him.

Unable to contain her emotions, Alice broke down at Percy's bedside. The weight of the years of searching and uncertainty finally lifted off her shoulders. "Oh, Peter!" she sobbed, reaching out to hold his hand. "I had to change my name so that horrid man wouldn't find me and ma."

"I changed mine too because I was scared." Percy looked at his sister as his eyes watered.

The two siblings sat there, a torrent of emotions washing over them. For years, they had each believed the other was lost forever, but now, fate had brought them back together.

As the hospital room filled with their shared emotions, Percy knew he had to explain his reasons for leaving. "Grace, can I call you that?" he began, his voice steady.

Grace nodded and smiled at her brother.

"I ran away because I was scared. I watched pa and that man fight. I saw pa fall against the wall and I watched you and ma run as quickly as possible. I was so afraid of what I saw, I ran back into the workhouse. I looked for you for days, but there was no sign of you."

Percy's sister stroked his hand lightly, her eyes locked onto his. "Oh Percy, we have so much to catch up on. I suppose I should call you Percy seeing that it is the name on your bed?"

Percy smiled and nodded slightly.

"I'm so sorry we didn't come back for you but we were terrified."

"You don't have to be sorry. It's more important we've found each other. And one day, I'll tell you everything." Percy felt a warmth spreading through him. For the first time in years, he allowed himself to feel the comfort of family love, the kind of love that can heal even the deepest wounds.

As the sun began to set outside the hospital window, Grace realised she needed to leave. "I have to go, Percy. Ma needs me," she said, determination in her voice.

"Why are you still here then?"

"Someone is stopping me."

"Who? Why would they do that?"

"He won't let me go, it's like he has a hold over me. But I have no choice. I must make him see sense." Grace's eyes began to water as she slipped her hand out of her brother's and turned to walk away. "I will explain, but I can't talk now. I will be back later when I've seen the other patients."

Percy watched his sister walk back down the ward. As he lay in his hospital bed, he couldn't help but wonder what life had in store for them next. With the knowledge that he had a loving sister by his side, he felt a newfound sense of hope and belonging. But he couldn't lie to himself. Percy was concerned for Grace. Who and why was someone stopping her from seeing her own mother?

Chapter Thirty-Three

The Adelphi performer reached out to Nancy with open arms, a reunion akin to a parent finding a lost child. With warmth in her voice, she spoke, kissing Nancy on each cheek, "You're truly one of my heroines."

Nancy found her anger quelled by Agnes's immediate response. The angry impulse she'd harboured earlier had somewhat subsided. She hadn't wanted to storm up to the star and cry 'Fraudster!' like she'd imagined when she left home. This shift caught Nancy off guard, her voice trembling as she spoke, "Well, it might sound odd, but I was hoping we could chat privately."

"Absolutely, my pleasure. What's on your mind?" Agnes's voice held a welcoming tone.

"Could we perhaps get something to eat? Nothing has passed my lips for hours and I'm famished."

Her stomach's rumble was a reminder; Nancy hadn't eaten since breakfast. Agnes nodded enthusiastically as they headed toward the Adelphi Theatre restaurant. Nancy checked the street both ways thrice before they crossed – She didn't want to come to the same demise as her former husband's grisly death.

"Fancy a West End star seeking help from me instead of the other way around." Agnes wore an air of joy, treating Nancy's spur-of-the-moment request as a grand gift. Eagerly, she followed the veteran toward the restaurant. The waiter recognised Nancy and led them to a prime table.

"Here you go, ladies. If you need anything, just let me know. What'll you have to drink?"

"Water for me, Cuthbert." Nancy looked at Agnes, waiting for her to tell the expectant waiter what she wanted to drink.

"How about champagne? I always think it's nice to celebrate after a performance," the charming waiter suggested.

Agnes didn't need a second invitation, eagerly agreeing with him. "I'm genuinely honoured, Nancy. You've asked me for help and brought me out for supper."

"Bit awkward, really. But I think you can put my mind at ease." Nancy glanced around, ensuring no curious ears were close. "You know I'm married to Percy Hartman, right?"

Agnes placed a comforting hand on Nancy's, her expression shifting from elation to compassion. "I do, Nancy. I heard about him being in the hospital. He's an extraordinary man; his valour that night deserves commendation."

Agnes's response wasn't quite what Nancy had expected. She'd half-anticipated scepticism, wondering if her suspicions were baseless. She was caught off guard. "So, you do know him well, then?"

"Who? Percy? Indeed. He was my music man for 'bout four years. Helped me shine. Then he moved on, thought I should find someone to take me higher. 'Made you a star, Agnes. Time for another to push your success!' I remember his words." Agnes gazed into the distance, lost in memory. "But it didn't go as planned. Couldn't find anyone like Hartman, and then we lost touch."

Nancy raised an eyebrow. "I never knew. When we met, he just said he'd written songs for you."

"Oh, yes. He composed my music. Fans adored it; he made me a true star. I'm forever grateful. But fame faded for a while after we parted."

"So, he wrote original music for you?"

Agnes fidgeted, avoiding Nancy's gaze. Nerves danced beneath her skin, noticed by Nancy.

"Thing is, Agnes, I played a song at my last performance. 'My Old Man Loves Me,' you know that one? It sounds uncannily similar to 'The Night He Left Me.'"

Agnes reddened, hands fumbling under the table. She picked at her fingernails nervously. "Is there a problem?"

Nancy sensed unease, butterflies stirring.

Agnes took a deep breath. "I'm sorry, Nancy. I never thought you'd find out."

Nancy's heart dropped. The possibility loomed that her world might unravel from a secret she might not want to unearth.

Chapter Thirty-Four

Nancy sat opposite Agnes, her gaze fixed expectantly, awaiting Agnes's revelation. Her fingers nervously sought refuge in her mouth, gnawing on what remained of her nails. "Go on," Nancy urged.

"I never meant for it to happen. You see, when Percy moved on, I struggled to find someone as skilled as him to compose my music," Agnes confessed, her eyes drifting into the distance. "I searched high and low, even falling prey to that trickster, Charles Chambers. He was a right one he was. Swindling me out of all my money. And he'd done it to others. How can they get away with it? He promised me fame and songs, took my money, but the music never surfaced. I was foolish to trust him."

Nancy's patience wore thin, her eagerness palpable. "Agnes, please, tell me."

"It was about ten months ago. Word got around that Percy was your agent after your husband passed. I confess, a twinge of envy flitted across me, seeing him paired with talent. I was disillusioned and thought I could coax him back to work for me. When I discovered you were rehearsing 'The Lights Of Home' at the Adelphi, I thought I might catch him there."

The show flashed vividly in Nancy's memory – the performance Percy had composed, garnishing her with glowing reviews.

Agnes's lips tightened as she continued her tale. "Summoning courage, I walked to the theatre hoping to speak to him. However, when I arrived at the theatre, it was deserted. You must have been on a break between rehearsals. I looked all around for you both but couldn't find you anywhere. So, I wandered to the piano, sat down, and my fingers danced across the keys. That's when I saw them – pages upon pages of sheet music, Percy's name scrawled in the corner."

A pang of unease swept through Agnes, bracing herself for Nancy's reaction.

"I leafed through the manuscript, fingers tracing the notes, and I started to sing the lyrics. It was as if I was entranced. The melody was enchanting, unlike anything I'd heard. I could picture myself on stage, captivating the audience with that song."

Nancy exhaled with relief. "So, someone did peruse his music that day! I thought he'd gone a bit peculiar, claiming someone had rummaged through his notes."

THE STARLET SLUM GIRL

A waiter arrived with two steaming plates and set them before the hungry women, who paid no heed to his presence, engrossed in their unfolding drama.

"What happened next?" Nancy inquired, her knife and fork poised, ready to devour her meal.

"I etched the first page into my memory, then, paper and pencil in hand, I hastily transcribed the notes before slipping away unnoticed. At home, I composed the rest of the song. To my astonishment, my fans adored it. The more they applauded, the more I sang it," Agnes admitted.

Nancy's laughter intermingled with her bites, prompting a quizzical frown from Agnes.

"Tell me, what's amusing you? I've fretted over this since the first time I sang the song. Stealing someone else's music, especially yours, was bound to catch up with me."

Nancy wiped a tear from her eye, her mirth unabated. "Agnes, I'm not laughing at you. I'm laughing at my own daftness."

Nancy's words took a moment to sink in for Agnes. "Wait, what? You're laughing at yourself? Why?"

Nancy leaned in, her voice lowered to a whisper. "I had this wild notion that Percy was plagiarising music. I don't even know why – exhaustion, perhaps. It's ludicrous to think he'd stoop so low." Drawing closer, almost brushing her food, she continued, "Promise not to tell, will you? I'd rather not see this splashed across the papers."

"Cross my heart, I won't! I'm relieved you're not about to sue me for thieving. I've been dreading the worst ever since I sang that song."

"We're quite a pair, aren't we?"

They chuckled as they concluded their meal, camaraderie blooming as if they'd been friends forever. Before bidding each other goodnight, Agnes laid a gentle hand on Nancy's arm.

"Listen, Percy's a gem of a fellow. Caring, selfless. He'd never harm a soul. Always puts others first."

Nancy recalled Percy's bravery, staying behind in the blazing theatre to rescue lives.

"You're lucky to have him, Nancy. Jealousy brews out there. Hold on to him, for he's the kindest soul you'll meet."

Nancy returned home that night, a contented smile on her lips. She knew Percy couldn't be a fraud, yet the missing money mystery beckoned her curiosity.

Chapter Thirty-Five

"Mrs Hartman, come and sit down."

Nancy hadn't bothered to find a doctor or nurse when she entered St Thomas' the following morning. Instead, she walked straight to the physician's office that she had sat in only six days previously.

The doctor paused for a moment and leaned back in his chair.

"Come on, doctor. Don't delay giving me the news. I want to know now. How is my husband? Is he going to survive?"

She thought she could feel her heart was about to burst through her chest because it beat so ferociously. Her right foot started tapping on the floor nervously, waiting for the doctor to continue.

"I'm pleased to say that Mr Hartman is showing good signs of recovery. He's sore and has raw burns, but he'll recover with proper medical care. I am confident he will pull through."

She started to cry tears of happiness. "Thank you, doctor, thank you so much. This is the best news ever!" She stood up and walked around to where the doctor was sitting, grabbed his cheeks between her hands and kissed him on his forehead.

Dr Miller went bright red. No need for that, Mrs Hartman. It's not every day a patient's relative gives me a kiss." The doctor shifted position in his seat, composing himself after feeling embarrassed by her sudden gesture.

"Oh, come on, Dr Miller, don't make too much of it. I'm a brazen performer. Always have been, always will be! Now, where is he? I want to see him."

Without further ado, they walked down the bare corridor whilst Nancy held her breath, trying to block the stench again.

As they reached the ward, the doctor turned to face Nancy.

"He's up on the left at the end. Please don't tell anyone about your visit. It's out of hours and—"

"Yes, yes, if everyone finds out, you will have a job on your hands."

He frowned at the actress.

"I know because the sister said the same thing to Percy when he visited me in the hospital."

"It seems like we need to tighten up our rules, don't we?" he said, giving her the biggest smile she had witnessed in days.

Nancy tentatively walked between the two lines of iron beds. Not wanting to look at how sick the other patients were, she nervously walked towards her husband, keeping her head down until she reached his bedside. She covered her mouth as if to stop herself from sobbing at the sight of him. He was covered in bandages from his neck down to his feet and lay on top of the cotton sheets to avoid any excessive pressure on his burns. He looked up as he recognised the familiar figure standing over him.

"Hello, my love."

"Oh, Percy! I can't decide if I'm pleased to see you alive or horrified at the state of you."

"Possibly a bit of both, hey?"

She nodded and took a seat on the wooden chair at his bedside.

As their eyes met, tears ran down their cheeks. They said nothing for a couple of minutes. They gazed into each other's eyes, love penetrating their souls.

"Oh, Nancy."

"Oh, Percy."

They said together.

"You go first."

"No, you."

"No, you, please."

"I never thought I would see you again, Nancy. This morning, I woke up in immense pain without knowing how long I had been here for."

Nancy pressed her lips together. She yearned to relieve his pain and restore normality, despite feeling hurt and confused about the theft from someone she loved. "I didn't know if you were alive or dead."

Percy wished his hand could break free from the bandages and encase it around hers.

"I'll help you, Percy, not out of obligation as your wife, but desire to see you well again. I want to take care of you so we can get back to doing shows together, walking in the park and making memories we will treasure forever."

"Me too, my love, me too," he said, as he noticed her gaze dropping slowly to the floor. "Hey, whatever is the matter, Nancy? I thought you would be pleased to see me. I can tell something is wrong."

Nancy felt nervous, but she had to find the courage within herself to ask about the money so they could put the past behind them and move on with nothing untoward hanging over their heads. "Percy, there's something I've been thinking about for a while. We need to talk to ensure there's nothing to worry about and focus on you getting better instead."

He wondered what was bothering his new wife. "What is it, Nancy? You know, you can ask me anything."

She regretted doubting the absence of the money. He sounded so sincere. How could she ever question his integrity? She took a deep breath. "The morning after the fire, I found there was no food in the house. I was hungry because I hadn't eaten for almost sixteen hours. The old tin in the desk drawer was empty when I went to get some money."

"That isn't anything to worry about, is it?"

"Not on its own, it wasn't. I went to the bank to withdraw some money from our account." She looked at him for signs of any nervous disposition, but there was nothing. "The bank clerk stated a balance of only five hundred pounds, despite me depositing all of the ticket sales. I knew that Robert had emptied the account previously. But just before you and I got together, the account was bursting at the seams." She noticed that Percy didn't flinch at what she had just told him. "The bank clerk told me you had withdrawn cash on sixteen occasions, each time leaving a balance of only five hundred pounds. I'm confused. Why would you do such a thing? Where has it all gone?"

"Oh Nancy, I'm so sorry. This is not how I wanted you to find out. I hope you can forgive me."

Chapter Thirty-Six

"Why would you do such a thing, Percy? After everything I've been through!" Nancy's cheeks started to burn, a lump forming at the back of her throat which she tried to gulp down.

"You don't honestly think that I would steal from you, do you? You are the love of my life, and from the moment I met you, I wanted to spend the rest of my days together with you in my arms. I was even prepared to fight over you because I wanted you so badly. It devastated me to witness how Robert was treating his wife. No man should ever treat his woman like that. I knew you deserved better."

"But where did the money go?"

"I told you a little lie on the night of the fire, Nancy. Do you remember asking me about the sale of the theatre, and I said the taxpayers had rebuked the London Metropolitan Borough?"

Nancy frowned as she thought back, trying to remember the conversation.

"Well, I offered to buy the theatre instead. I made the owner an offer he couldn't refuse, and we signed the contracts a few days before the fire after we got back from our honeymoon."

"What? So—let me get this straight. Do you own the Cambridge Theatre? Well, what's left of it?"

"No, Nancy, we own it! As soon as I signed the sale contract, I immediately had it transferred into joint property rights between the two of us. It's our theatre. I intended the night I took you to the show to be celebratory, not disastrous. It was to celebrate us being the new owners of the Cambridge Theatre."

She didn't know whether to laugh or cry. Her eyes were wide, trying to comprehend what he had just told her.

"Oh Percy, why did I think the worst of you?"

"You didn't think I'd steal your money, did you, Nancy?"

"I won't lie. It did cross my mind."

"You silly thing. Why would I do that? No, you, and I are the proud owners of the Cambridge Theatre."

"But it's burned to the ground, Percy! What are we going to do? We have no money to rebuild it."

"Yes, we do. Because the owner cut his losses and ran, I negotiated him down to a rock-bottom price for the deal. We have enough money left over to rebuild it. How does that sound?"

"Percy, I'm so annoyed that you never told me, but equally, I am absolutely elated that you could have done such a thing for us."

"Our future is all I think about. Nancy, you really are my everything."

Nancy's eyes welled up with tears again. Leaning over the chair, she retrieved her handkerchief from her bag on the floor.

"Why the tears, Nancy? I thought you would be happy."

"Oh, I am, Percy. But there's more. I hope you will be as happy as I am about it."

She looked down at her stomach and stroked it. Percy's gaze looked towards her hands, and a smile formed across his face.

"Oh, my goodness, Nancy, you are, aren't you?"

She smiled and nodded.

"Yes, I am. If your hands weren't bandaged, I would grab them and place them here," she said, pointing to her stomach. "It's true, my love. We are expecting our first child!"

It was Percy's turn to shed tears.

"It's all I've ever wanted, Nancy. We are going to be wonderful parents."

Nancy stood up and leant over her husband and kissed him fiercely on the lips, heedless of onlookers. "I hope so, Percy. But I want no more secrets between us."

Percy's expression drooped, and he sighed. The bed sheets moving in synchronicity with his chest.

"Percy, what's the matter?"

He looked at the expectant performer sitting beside him, knowing that what he was about to say would change the family dynamics forever. "I have something else to tell you, Nancy."

Nancy's heart skipped a beat, the feeling of butterflies fluttered in her stomach. She took a deep breath in and held it for a couple of seconds. "What is it? Should I be concerned?"

"No, no! At least, I don't think so."

"Don't keep me waiting. Has it got anything to do with how close you were with that nurse when I walked in?"

"Kind of, but don't be alarmed."

Nancy sucked in her cheeks, her mouth pouting.

"The thing is, I know that nurse."

"I was right! When I walked in I thought you were both far too close just to be nurse and patient," Nancy stood up, pushing the chair back so the legs scraped along the wooden floor. Percy winced at the noise, and then the ward fell silent.

"Nancy, sit down, please."

She slowly sat down and pulled the chair a little closer again.

"Remember me saying I haven't seen my sister in years? I suppose I gave up finding her."

"Go on."

Percy beamed with joy. "She's here, Nancy. Right here in the hospital. I found Grace."

Chapter Thirty-Seven

The grey skies outside were heavy and sombre, prompting the nurses to light the ward's gas lamps. The soft, warm glow from the lamps provided a gentle contrast to the harsh reality faced by the patients. Rain beat relentlessly against the large windows, creating a soothing backdrop.

By Percy's bedside, Nancy's presence cast a reassuring light. His tired eyes met hers, brimming with gratitude. He wrestled with the right moment to share his thoughts, feeling a sense of security in his future with Nancy.

Nancy's expression was one of quiet encouragement, inviting Percy to break the silence after his revelation.

"Nancy," he began, his voice was fragile. "Are you pleased?"

Nancy's eyes widened with curiosity, her surprise clear in Percy's earnest tone. She shifted in her chair, her attention wholly on him. "Yes, of course I am. But, last time you spoke of her, you hadn't seen her or your ma in years."

"I know. I'm as surprised as you are."

"Where is she? How did you cross paths?"

"Here on this ward, she is a nurse."

"Percy, it's a wonderful—"

Grace approached his bed and Nancy's words were cut short. Holding a thermometer, her cheeks tinged with a blush, Grace cleared her throat with a hint of embarrassment. "Oh, I didn't mean to intrude," Grace murmured, her voice gentle and a tad sheepish.

Percy's smile was warm, his concern clear. "No intrusion at all, Grace. Please, allow me to introduce you to Nancy."

As Grace came closer, Percy introduced her to his wife, their gazes locking with a hint of recognition.

"Nancy, this is Grace, my sister," Percy's voice brimmed with warmth. "Grace, my wife, Nancy."

Nancy extended a friendly smile. "I'm confused. I've known you as Alice whilst you have been looking after my husband."

"We had to change our names, our lives were in danger in very different ways." Grace bowed her head and gazed towards the floor.

"I understand," Nancy said. "It must have been terrible for you all."

Percy looked at his sister and his concern peaked. "What's the matter, Grace?"

"I'm still bothered by Archie's letter. Our ma appears to be sick, and he says she may not pull through."

Nancy frowned. "Then why are you still here? You should go see her."

"Jeremy disagrees," Grace's eyes glistened.

"Who is Jeremy?"

"He is a doctor here—he, he is also my beau."

"Jeremy should want what's best for you, not just himself."

A blush tinted Grace's cheeks as her gaze dropped.

"Sorry, perhaps that's too much. But trust me. If he truly loves you, he'd support what's best for you."

Percy nodded in agreement, smiling at his sister.

"Grace, family matters most," Nancy added gently. "Your ma needs you now. Don't let fear or duties stop you from seeing her. You will regret it forever if she dies."

Grace's eyes welled, a mix of gratitude and unease in her gaze.

With a trembling voice, Nancy continued, emotions raw. "I've felt the pain of missed chances, not being there for loved ones. Don't repeat it, Grace. Time with your mother is precious."

Tears streaked Grace's cheeks, her inner turmoil visible. "But what if I lose everything? What if I lose him?"

Nancy's gaze burned, her voice fervent. "Grace, love shouldn't hold you back from where you're needed. You can bridge the gap, but not the lost time with your mother."

Grace's eyes moved from Nancy to Percy, his agreement unspoken but palpable. Grace wiped her tears, determination and sadness intertwining. "What about Percy, we've only just been reunited. And now there is you too, Nancy. It's like having a second family to consider."

Nancy and Percy exchanged a glance, understanding unspoken.

"Go to her, Grace. Percy and I will still be here when you return. We can get to know each other properly when you have seen your ma, but right now, she is more important than anybody else."

Grace's shoulders dropped, and she sighed with relief. She no longer had the burden of the decision. "You're right. I must go. Thank you for showing me what matters."

As Grace left, Percy turned to Nancy, his voice carrying past regrets. "Thank you, Nancy, for reminding us."

Nancy's eyes shimmered, heart echoing his sentiment. "What do you mean?"

"Reminding us what is important. The past few days have shown us all what really matters. We can't ever risk losing that again."

"Family is a treasure, Percy. We must cherish it."

In the dim ward, the rain continued to lash against the windows. The gas lights glowed to illuminate the rows of beds and the patients lying within them. Nancy's whispers would stay with Percy forever as they shared an understanding which now bound them. A testament to love's value.

Chapter Thirty-Eight

Percy's road to recovery was lit by a single beacon - the image of Nancy, carrying their unborn child. He could recall that day when she had revealed the news in languid tones, his body still chained to the hospital bed. His eyes had shone with tears as they clung to each other's lips. Their public display of affection had been a vow; an unspoken pledge of the strength that bound them together.

The carriage navigated the narrow cobbled streets, weaving around rough holes in the road and other carriages carrying their passengers. The journey was testament to his desire to be by his wife's side as she gave birth to their first child. Each bump in the road brought a grunt of surprise from him, which translated into gritted teeth and tighter grips on the handle.

"Percy! What are you doing here?"

Although the carriage had dropped him at the door, the rain was so heavy and persistent, his hair looked like it was glued to his head, tiny droplets of rain hanging from the ends of his dark hair. "Are you going to let me in?" He held an arm across his waist, his other tucked inside his jacket to keep the dressings dry.

Nancy's expression softened as she looked at him, taking in his battered appearance and the clear effort it had taken for him to make his own way home. She rushed forward to take his arm, and helping him up the steps. Once inside, she tenderly helped him out of his damp coat.

"I can't believe you're here!" she exclaimed, as he stumbled slightly on his way to the nearest chair. "How did you even manage it?"

Percy gave a weak smile, feeling like he'd been hit by a sledgehammer from the effort of coming all this way. "I had to see my wife, you are carrying my child so it's important I help you as much as you have me. Nothing was going to stop me."

Nancy's smile turned tender as she took his hand in hers, feeling the rough edges of his healing wounds and the callouses that had built up on his palms. "You're amazing. You know that? I don't think I've ever loved you more than I do right now."

Percy leaned forward to press his lips to hers, feeling the heat between them grow instantly. Even though he was exhausted and still in pain, he couldn't help but let Nancy know just how much he loved her. He pulled back with a grin as she pouted playfully.

"I missed you," she murmured, trailing her fingers over his stubbled chin.

"I missed you too," Percy replied huskily. "We also have our child to think about now, don't we?"

Nancy's eyes widened with excitement as she remembered their impending new arrival. "Yes! Yes, we do! Oh, Percy—"

"Shh, we can talk more later. For now, just let me feel." He tenderly placed his hand on Nancy's pregnant bump, feeling a slight kick from their child."

"Hey, don't cry, unless they are happy tears."

"Yes, they are. I never thought I was going to leave that place. Dr Miller kept insisting I had to stay."

"That doesn't surprise me. By the way, have you heard if Jeremy is looking for Grace?"

Percy shook his head. "No, nothing. The last I heard was that he had found her note, but as far as I am aware he hasn't gone after her."

Nancy gave a wry smile. "That's good. Come, let's have some tea."

Percy's eyes widened with delight as he walked into the drawing room. "The tree looks beautiful. Next year I can help."

I decorated it to distract myself from missing you. It's been lonely here on my own." Nancy had hung the decorations from the branches, carefully placing each one until she was happy with the finished tree. She bought another one for the parlour to chase away his absence.

When Percy looked around the room, he smiled as he saw the framed photos from their honeymoon.

"They were expensive but worth it," she said, as if answering the question in his mind. "Let's not worry about money, it will come as soon as we release the first show. Which reminds me, we have a visitor coming on New Year's Eve."

"Oh, who is that?"

"His name is Jack."

"Oh? How did you meet him?" A pang of jealousy stung the back of Percy's throat.

"Don't look like that, you are my only beau. Besides, he's way too young for me," she said playfully.

"So, how did you meet him?"

"I haven't yet. Leo has invited him. He knows him through Cecil, the gentleman who makes Leo's suits and provides the materials for my costumes. Apparently Jack is Cecil's nephew and has the voice on an angel."

"Can he not come and audition at the theatre?"

"Afraid not. He suffers from nerves so the only way Leo is managing to get him to audition is by inviting Cecil and his related family to ours on New Year's Eve. I have to pretend that our entertainer pulled out last minute."

"Okay, well, I supposed a bit of light entertainment will brighten up the place for our guests."

"Leo thinks this Jack will be the lead role in our new show."

"New show? The theatre is still a pile of ashes."

"Not for long, my love. But first, let's celebrate Christmas and New Year and then we can think about the theatre and performances."

Percy smiled at his wife wondering what she had been up to whilst he had been recovering in hospital.

Chapter Thirty-Nine

"Where are they then? They should be here by now." Nancy glanced at the grandfather clock in the corner of the room. It had just gone eight, and the guests were getting restless for some entertainment.

Nancy wanted this New Year's Eve to be perfect after the dramas of the past twelve months. She was adamant that her and Percy would have a good year ahead, and that meant for the night to go without unexpected delays or incidents.

"Stop panicking, he will be here, Nancy. I promise." Leo smiled then turned on his heels, almost spilling the golden liquid from the champagne coupe.

Nancy watched him mingling and smiled at her ever faithful and committed friend.

A knock came from the front door. It was barely audible amidst the background noise of conversation and a phonograph playing. Nancy admired the extra hired staff filling glasses and walking amongst her friends and family with canapés.

Nancy glanced up and noticed Leo leading a crowd of people into the room.

"They're here! They're here!" Leo exclaimed once again throwing his arm in the air, causing champagne to recklessly spill over the side of the coupe.

"You must be Mr Cavendish, it's so good to meet you," Leo said. "Come this way, come and meet Nancy."

"I hope it's all been good, Leo, and my daughter hasn't been blackening my name," George shouted above the noise in the drawing room.

Leo ignored him and walked straight to Nancy, with Clara, Jack, George, and Cecil following closely behind.

Jack glanced to the front of the room and noticed the lid on the grand piano was open and waiting for its performer to bring the ebony black and white keys to life. He sucked in his cheeks slightly and looked around, wondering who would be playing.

Clara pretended not to notice how nervous her beau looked.

"Leo! Why don't you introduce us?" Nancy said as she walked over to her best friend. The champagne in her glass sparkled against the lights, the bubbles floating in the gold-coloured liquid.

"This is Jack, the singer, I keep telling you about him."

"So you're our stand in entertainer for this evening," Nancy said, holding her hand out to shake Jack's. It's good to meet you at last. Leo tells me you have a powerful voice."

"Stand in entertainer? Nobody told me about that?" Jack looked at Clara. "Did you have anything to do with this?"

"Excuse me, I must go and powder my nose." Clara swiftly left the room, leaving Leo to explain what had happened.

"She's not entirely to blame, Jack. I agreed to it when she asked. All in the name of helping you onto the stage."

"But, Leo, I told her I wasn't ready!"

"Jack, listen to me," Nancy said, putting on her best warm smile. "You have nothing to be nervous about. If what Leo says is true, you will be better than the entertainer we hired anyway. Simply follow the music and sing along."

"I—I'm sorry, I can't do it." Jack rubbed the back of his neck and beads of sweat formed on his brow. His eyes wandered around the room. The strangers, drinking and being merry, stared back at him. A hundred eyes were upon him.

"Jack you're sweating, are you okay?" Cecil put a loving hand on his shoulder.

"No, no, I'm not. This is too much, I'm sorry." He shoved the glass of champagne they gave him on arrival towards George, who had no choice but to take the glass from him.

"Jack! Where are you going? Everybody is waiting!"

"Oh dear, looks like your man has changed his mind. That's a shame. I was looking forward to hearing him sing. He may have had a chance to audition. And Clara will learn. It never does a woman any good to chase after a man," Nancy said.

"I do apologise, Mrs Hartman, he really does suffer with his nerves," George said, whilst shifting from foot to foot.

"Well he needs to do something about that if he has any chance of being on stage. And please, call me Nancy. None of this formal stuff where I come from."

"Nancy Franklin. I finally get to meet you. I'm Cecil Dalton, the gentleman who supplies all the material for your costumes."

"Ah, so you're the one who is responsible for my feather fetish then, it's lovely to meet you. Leo comes back from your store and gives me all the details and gossip from his visits. It's quite the place I believe."

"You could say that, I've been doing it for so long I have quite the collection for Leo to choose from."

"Well I hope you will be making costumes for Jack soon too if his voice lives up to Leo's praises."

Cecil rolled his eyes. "And that's if he comes back, he is so dramatic sometimes."

"He's in the right place then isn't he?" Nancy said followed by a laugh so loud and infectious, the crowd stood around her couldn't help but join in.

"Jack! Clara! We didn't think you would come back, did we, George?" Cecil said. "I for one am glad you are here."

"Look at me. My hair is bedraggled and I feel a mess."

"You are still beautiful to me, Clara."

"Did I hear someone say they look bedraggled? We can't have that on New Year's Eve, can we?" Nancy walked over to Clara. "Jessica? Take Clara to get cleaned up. I'm sure she will feel much better when you have helped her tidy herself up."

"Thank you, Nancy, I didn't expect that."

"It's my pleasure." As Nancy watched her maid take Clara to freshen up, she spoke to Jack. "You need to overcome your nerves, Jack, if you are ever going to perform."

"I know, I'm sorry. It's been a long time since I sang in front of a big crowd. Maybe it's because my pa always laughed at me and told me to stop being a wussy." Jack's eyes glazed over.

"Well that won't have helped." Nancy touched Jack's forearm. "You will be fine, I promise. Come with me."

Nancy led Jack to the front of the room and stood by the piano. "Now then. This young man 'ere is a bit nervous. He's been asked to perform at short notice, but his shyness gets the better of him. So if we're all going to have a good night into the early hours, I suggest we give him our support. "'Ere," Nancy said, passing Jack a crystal low ball of brandy. Have a gulp of this and sing to your 'earts content me lad."

Jack raised his glass, knocked the drink back in one, and opened his mouth. He urged his voice to fill the room with gentle notes as the whole room was quiet, waiting expectantly. But nothing came out.

Nancy looked at him and nodded encouragingly. "Why don't I help?" The star whispered. She moved closer to him and started singing.

As Jack duetted with Nancy Franklin, the biggest star on the London show scene, he couldn't believe how relaxed he started to feel.

Nancy smiled at the young starlet and continued for another three songs. As soon as they finished, Leo walked to the front and passed him a crystal glass of whiskey. Jack knocked the amber liquid back in three gulps.

"Jack, Leo said you had a good voice, but I didn't expect that." You remind me of myself when I was your age. I had a bit more courage than you, though.

Blushing, Jack looked down at the glass in his hands, searching for something suitable to say to the performer.

"It seems to me, Jack, you just need a bit more courage. Once you have a few performances, I promise you'll come through," Nancy said.

"Who knows when that will be, I'm sure there are better performers out there."

"Nonsense! I won't have you saying that. You have a wonderful voice," Nancy gave the shy singer an encouraging smile. "So, how about it, then?"

"What? How about what?"

"You, silly. I need a main man for the leading role in my next show. You up for it?"

"Yes! Yes, he is." Clara said.

"Clara, where did you come from?"

"Jessica helped me clean up a little, I need to look my best for you, don't I?"

Nancy rolled her eyes at Clara. "You still have a lot to learn about men Miss Cavendish. Now, where were we? Do you want the part or not? Last chance."

Jack looked at Clara, George, and Cecil, each in turn. He knew he had no choice if he was to marry Clara, she meant everything to him. "Yes I do, thank you."

"Finally! They all said together, lifting their glasses in celebration.

Epilogue

Percy looked at Nancy with adoring eyes, wondering what he had done to deserve such a caring woman who pursued everything in her life with such ambition and determination. It made him proud, and the night they went to see 'Haste To The Wedding' he was so happy to show off to the world that he was her husband.

"No, silly, don't put those there. They will look better here!"

The last few days before the grand opening were tense. Lilly was teething and crawling, so she needed the care and attention from her mother. Percy did the best he could nursing the wriggling child without putting too much pressure on his scars. He looked at his wife, ordering people around inside the theatre, making sure everything was perfect. Percy gazed up at the ceiling from where he was sitting and thought that he couldn't have designed anything better himself. The ceiling roses were highlighted with gold leaf, from which three chandeliers hung magnificently, just like they had in the original building.

It took all his strength not to allow the memories of that fateful night to turn into a panic attack. Just as he thought his breathing might get out of control, he felt a tender hand on his shoulder and a kiss on his right cheek.

"Alright, my love?" Nancy said, taking their daughter from him.

"I am now."

Nancy watched her husband smile at their child and knew that he wished he could hold her for longer. But Lilly was starting to wriggle around more, impatient to get on the floor and crawl. She unintentionally hurt his tender, pink flesh.

"Please don't ever be afraid of handing her to me, Nancy. I want to be a big part of her life. That means holding her as much as I can. It might hurt a little, but it's worth it."

"I wonder if she will become a star, just like her mother?"

"Of course, she will. I can just tell she will follow in your footsteps."

"Oi, not here, over there! How many times do I have to tell you?"

"That's a little harsh, isn't it, Nancy?"

"Maybe so, but if I don't keep them on their feet, then we will never be ready! Excuse me for a minute. I need to go and check if they've put enough champagne flutes out on the table."

Nancy handed Lilly back to her pa and disappeared into a wave of people placing flowers, champagne flutes, chairs, and tables in all the right places. She wanted the evening to be perfect, and quite rightly so.

This was their future, and she had worked hard to make sure the opening night would go as planned. She knew she would be busy during the day with no time to head home and change, so she brought her outfit for the evening to the dressing room. When she was satisfied that everything was as perfect as it could be, and the organisers had left the theatre, she went to get changed.

Sat humming to herself in front of the mirror, she applied her make-up and pinned her hair up in curls on top of her head. Looking from side to side, she felt nerves in her tummy. *My goodness, I feel as if I'm about to perform!*

"You are!"

She looked behind her in the mirror to see Leo standing in the doorway.

"Leo! I thought I was talking to myself." She stood up and walked over to give him a hug.

"You were. It's just that I was listening."

"You're early. Have you come to help me look presentable?" She smiled at her best friend, who was looking smart in a burgundy velvet jacket, white shirt, black trousers, and a matching bow tie.

"Actually, now you have come to mention it, I have. I have also brought you a gift to wear."

"Oh Leo, you shouldn't have. Just standing by me after everything I've been through is the biggest gift a friend could ask for."

He brought his hands from behind his back and gave her a black velvet square box, dressed with a bright pink ribbon.

"Aw, Leo, bright pink. My favourite colour! It reminds me of that costume you made for me a couple of years back."

She flipped back the lid of the box to reveal a single row of dress diamonds on a headband.

"Here, let me."

He took the piece of dress jewellery out of the box and placed it in front of the mound of dark brown curls piled high on Nancy's head.

She touched either side of the headband and looked at it from all angles with a bright smile on her face. "It's stunning, Leo. Thank you."

"I'm sorry they're not real, as you can probably gather, but they look genuine and will last for a long time."

"The value isn't important, Leo. It's the thought that counts."

"It sure is, my love."

Percy had walked into the dressing room, clumsily holding Lilly-Rose in his arms, overhearing the end of the conversation.

"Oh here, Percy, let me take her off you."

He gave his daughter to her Uncle Leo. "Thanks, Leo, my arms were getting a bit tired. I have one more thing to do for my wife before she cuts that beautiful red ribbon on the front door before her waiting fans."

Nancy looked at him curiously.

"Oh yeah, what might that be?"

"You forgot this, Nancy, and your neck is looking rather bare." He struggled to pull out the box from the inside of his jacket pocket. He put it down on the dressing table, and Nancy gasped a little.

"Oh, Percy, you remembered! Thank you so much. I had accidentally left them on the dressing table at home but didn't have time to go back and collect them."

His scarred hands fumbled to grasp hold of the string of pearls to fasten them around his wife's neck. He was determined to do this one thing for her as a token of his love and appreciation for all her hard work and commitment. But mostly, her love and dedication she had shown in helping him recover from the terrible ordeal.

The dressing room was silent as Nancy and Leo watched how much effort he put into lifting the string of pearls out of the box, then trying to get a grip on the clasp.

Neither of the two friends rushed him by interrupting asking if they could help. They both knew how important it was for him to carry out such a small, yet significant gesture for his wife. They waited patiently until finally, he stepped behind her and fastened the jewellery around her neck, finishing with a tender kiss on her skin.

"Oh, Percy, I love you," she said, touching the pearls with both hands.

"Right, you two, enough of that. Come on, you have work to do. Your fans are waiting for you to cut that ribbon, Nancy. I will carry this little one whilst you follow, and we'll meet you outside."

Leo carried Lilly out of the room and made her giggle and coo by tickling her under the chin.

Percy looked at his wife.

"May I?"

Nancy linked onto his arm, and they walked through the theatre one last time before its grand opening.

"Isn't it beautiful, Percy? Your dream has come true."

"All thanks to you, Nancy. You have done such a wonderful job overseeing the rebuilding of such a wonderful theatre."

"I can't wait for the first show to start, Percy. We only have three months, but I think we might just be able to do it."

"Of course, we will, my love. You are capable of anything. I have complete and utter faith in you. Let's go and tell the crowd when the first show is. I know they will be excited."

They made their way out of the front of the theatre and were confronted by a sea of fans who cheered and clapped loudly as the couple appeared in front of the theatre.

Nancy spotted her family at the front of the crowd and blew them a kiss.

The longer the couple stood in silence, the more the crowd roared, hoping it would speed up the opening ceremony.

Nancy felt like a real star. This was different to what she always felt on stage at the end of a performance. This was recognition of her hard work in reopening the theatre. This time she hadn't just simply shown up on the opening night. She had made the whole thing happen.

Percy tried to shush the crowds by holding his hands out in front of him and moving them up and down. '*Shhh,*' he mouthed as the noise dissipated quickly. He waited until it was deathly quiet.

"Now then, everybody. Can I have your attention, please? As you all know, the building that was here before what we are standing in front of today was reduced by a blazing inferno. It was a night where, sadly, three people lost their lives, and many more have been affected forever." He looked at his wife and gave her a comforting smile. "Nancy and I were here that evening, as you know, and I can tell you that the memories have been etched on our minds forever." Percy noticed a couple of spectators in the crowd starting to cry.

The poor souls, I bet they were there that night too. Nancy pondered as she witnessed some of the crowd bowing their heads and wiping tears away with their handkerchiefs.

"It is a night I would rather forget, but at the same time, remember for the rest of my life as I stand here in front of the new theatre that my wonderful wife Nancy has spent so much time seeing to the rebuild."

The crowd cheered again and raised their hands in the air. They started clapping and shouting out their appreciation for Nancy's hard work.

"I just want you all to know that I'm proud to be her husband, and I have watched her work tirelessly day in and day out to make sure the theatre is open and ready today. Not only that, but we can't wait to put on the first show for you in three months' time. My wife will not only be directing the performance, but she will also be hosting the auditions and deciding who plays a part in the show that we have written together. So, without further ado, please, Nancy Franklin, will you cut the ribbon to signify the opening of the Cambridge and Hartman Theatre!"

Percy handed his wife a pair of scissors. She held the ribbon between her forefinger and thumb and cut through it neatly and quickly.

The fans cheered as the scissors sliced through the red material and the ends fell to the floor. She grabbed hold of her husband around his waist, and he carefully placed his arms around her neck.

"I love you, Mrs Hartman."

"And I love you too, Percy."

The fans cheered and roared, then stopped when they saw Percy turn to face them again.

"One more thing," he said. Suddenly, Percy punched his fist into the air. "The show must go on!" He shouted gleefully.

Three days after the celebratory opening of the theatre, the auditions started. They had just a week to finalise the cast.

"This is so tiring. We have Jack as the male lead, but as for the rest?" Nancy shrugged her shoulders at her husband.

"Don't worry, it will all come together, you'll see."

Nancy took their beloved daughter from her husband whilst he continued calling the names out of the list of auditions.

"Okay, let's continue, shall we?"

Percy looked down at the handwritten list in front of him.

"Next!" Nancy shouted at the top of her voice. Both Percy and Nancy were so occupied with Lilly-Rose that they didn't see the person walking onto the stage. "Name?" Nancy called whilst wiping some dribble from Lilly-Rose's chin.

"Grace Hartman."

Suddenly, both Percy and Nancy looked up. Their eyes widened and sparkled as their mouths hung open.

"Grace? Oh Grace!"

Grace ran down the steps from the stage and hugged her brother. Tears of happiness fell from her eyes and landed on Percy's shoulder.

"And who is this?" Grace said, stepping back and admiring Lilly-Rose in her father's arms.

"Meet Lilly-Rose. Beautiful isn't she?" Nancy responded.

"Grace, but—what are you doing here? Are you here to audition?"

"No, silly. I thought it would be a nice surprise for you both to see me. So I put my name down to audition. I can't sing whatsoever."

"So, tell me, how is ma? I haven't heard anything from you. I was assuming the worst."

"I'm absolutely fine, dearest Percy."

Percy looked over his shoulder to where the voice was coming from. "Ma? Is that really you?"

"Oh, ma. I thought I had lost you forever." Percy passed Lilly to his wife then walked up to his long lost ma and wrapped his arms around her neck.

"I've missed you so much, Percy, I really have."

"How did you know I changed my name?"

"Grace told me everything, son. Absolutely everything."

THE END

About the Author

The next book in the series is out now, **The Lost Girl's Miracle**, you can download it here: https://mybook.to/LostGirlsMiracle

My free book, **The Whitechapel Angel**, is also available for download here: https://dl.bookfunnel.com/xs5p4d0oog

About the Author:

I have always been passionate about historical romance set in the Victorian era. I love to place myself on the dark, murky streets of London and wonder what it would have been like to overcome tragedy and poverty to find true love. The different classes of society intrigue me and I'm fascinated to know if love ever truly prevailed between the working and upper class.

I'm not sure about you, but whenever I visit the streets of Whitechapel, or read historical books from the bygone era, I find myself transported back to a time when I once lived there myself. Some say past lives are a myth, past life transgression is a 'load of tosh,' and you only ever live this life in the now. But whether you believe in past lives or not, for me, I easily feel myself living in those times.

With each book, I strive to create stories that capture the heart and imagination of my readers, bringing to life the strong, resilient characters that live in that bygone era.

When not writing, I can be found exploring the great outdoors with my husband Mike, and my Jack Russell, Daisy, or curled up with a good book. There is nothing quite like lighting the log burner and a candle or two, and turning the pages.

Stay connected:

Please, if you have any feedback, email me at anneliesemmckay@gmail.com (my admin assistant,) and I will respond to all of you personally.

Printed in Great Britain
by Amazon